Be Free

Be Free

TS Woolard

The Southern Tale Spinner

Dark Moon Rising Publications| Virginia

Dark Moon Rising Publications

70 Foxwood Drive
Rocky Mount, Virginia 24151
Tel: (540) 257-2861

Any and all characters are a work of fiction

Copyright © 2020 T.S. Woolard
Copyright © 2020 Dark Moon Rising Publications
All rights reserved.

ISBN-13: 978-1-945987-75-5

10 9 8 7 6 5 4 3 2 1

All rights reserved. No part of this publication may be reproduced, distributed, or transmitted in any form or by any means, including photocopying, recording, or other electronic or mechanical methods, without the prior written permission of the publisher, except in the case of brief quotations embodied in critical reviews and certain other noncommercial uses permitted by copyright law.
For permission requests, write to the publisher, addressed "Attention: Permissions Coordinator."

Printed in the United States of America

Other works by T.S. Woolard

Novels

The Meaning of Hell

Novellas

Heaven's Healer from Hell

Short Story Collections

Solo Circus

Psycho Circus

Poetry Collections

Sugar and Cyanide

Anthologies

Reject for Content 4: Highway to Hell

Lovecraft After Dark

Straight to Video: An Anthology of B-Movie Awesomeness

Horror From the Inside Out

The Grays

Undead Legacy

Beyond the Cosmic Veil

Urban Legends: Emergence of Fear

Fearotica: An Anthology of Erotic Horror

Ghosts: Revenge

Memento Mori: Remember You Will Die

Demonic Possession

Indiana Horror Review 2013

Indiana Horror Review 2014

Cellar Door III & Hell II: a Double Anthology

Suburban Secrets: a Neighborhood of Nightmares.

Suburban Secrets II: Graveyards and Cemeteries

Bones II

Serial Killers Quattuor
Fata Arcana
Full Moon Slaughter
M vs. F
VS
VS: X: US vs UK Extreme Horror
Anthology House's Big Book of Poetry
Ugly Babies III/ Ghosts Redemption
Midnight Remains
Season's Bleedings
Doorway to Death: An Anthology from the Other Side
Indiana Horror Review 2016
Floppy Shoes Apocalypse
Trashed
Kaiju: Lords of the Earth
Down the Rabbit Hole: Tales of Insanity

Ezines
Sirens Call eZine # 17,18,19,22, and 40

COMING SOON
Nectar and Napalm poetry collection

It wasn't a cult. Arthur got pissed off every time someone tried to say it was. He liked to refer to it as an *alternative devotion lifestyle.*

People from all over the world tried to run his little colony down. It bothered Arthur, and he was ever vigilant when it came to allowing his members online. It had been strictly banned. Evil came through the world wide web. The outside world didn't understand his and the colony's desire for the detachment from them. The truth seemed so easy to see once he became awakened.

Since that moment, Arthur made it his life's mission to spread his teachings as far as they could reach. Over time, he ended up in an old, abandoned asylum in west Africa. Over a hundred and thirty members of the group lived within its walls. Each person had their own room.

The men were expected to keep up the maintenance on the building. They took sole responsibility for repairing the place to an inhabitable state. Months were spent tearing out and replacing walls and floors. Painting and lying tile were done after.

The women were charged with growing the food, cooking, and cleaning up after the men. A female's place was to be subservient to a male. There was no other way around it. In the colony, there would be no discussing it, either.

Arthur hated women for the majority of his life. They were the devil's creation and were sent to the Earth to tempt otherwise brilliant and caring individuals—man. Women brought with them sex, headaches, and stress. A man could reach his full potential in God's eyes without the course-altering injection of a woman. Any time she got involved, she would cloud a man's mind with her own desires, and that only kept him from growing into his true self. He became the perfect man in her image, not God's, and that was strongly discouraged.

Women had their worth. They weren't trash. They were not something to be tossed aside and never acknowledged or interacted with. They were the most expendable form of human, though. Race, origin, and creed were not as important as gender. Your sex was the strongest determining factor in classification in the colony, and it was no secret to anyone.

In the very beginning, Arthur made it plain that women were only there to serve man. It was their duty to God for being born. There was no advancement in power because that was the highest power they could reach.

Abstinence was another one of Arthur's strict preachings, and it would be enforced by any means necessary. There was no play in that rule.

That rule was being tested. Arthur wasn't

happy.

Jerry and Rose were caught in the bathroom engaging in their primal urges. One of the higher-ups in the colony, Henry, found them after hearing the panting and stressed grunts on the fourth floor of the building. Few ever went up there, but Henry had noticed over the last few weeks they went missing around 3:30pm every day. He searched for them after realizing the strange development in their schedule and investigated covertly.

Rose should've been tending to the east garden at that time, and Jerry was supposed to be on break in the woodworking shop in the back, which used to be the loading dock for food shipments when the asylum was up and running. It was located on the east side of the building, as well. Neither were where they were instructed to be. That wouldn't be tolerated.

Henry first noticed Rose missing and thought maybe she had fallen ill or something. He went to check on her to make sure she was okay. The closest place he could ask about her—from someone reliable (not a woman)—was in the wood shop. He asked around among the guys there and noted Jerry's absence.

Coincidence, he thought. *No need to jump to conclusions when it was just one moment in one day. It may not mean anything.*

The next two days, the pair were where they were supposed to be, but on the third day, they were missing again. Same time, same circumstances.

Could it be two coincidences in the same week? That was highly unlikely, but still, Henry was reluctant to make that jump with one of his brother's wellbeing at stake.

The third time it happened, and second day in a row, Henry no longer cared about moving too fast on the spot. It was obvious what was going on.

He was disappointed in Jerry. At one time, Jerry was one of his close friends. He'd even talked to Arthur about moving him into guard in the future. Then, one night over a few glasses of homemade wine, Jerry let it slip that he sat on a substantial stack of porn magazines. That sort of weakness wouldn't make a good guard. He could stick to woodworking, and being Henry's sad, sinning friend.

With the new development, it seemed his old pal was backsliding further than he would've ever imagined. Henry struggled with not telling Arthur for the porn. He prayed for him at services, hoping his desires and sinning ways would leave his earthly body in time.

It hadn't worked, though. For most people,

that would signify the ineptitude of whatever deity they worshiped and sent requests to. For Henry, it just proved how correct Arthur had been about the evil women presented to even the best of men.

Henry went on a quiet search, never telling anyone what he caught on to. He hoped Jerry and Rose's little affair would run its course before he found them acting on their impulses. Then, it could be a situation where he couldn't prove anything, so there was no need to press it. Almost a don't ask/don't tell scenario.

As the weeks of the same thing happening went by, Henry's anger ate him alive. He blamed himself for enabling the whole thing. He should've turned him in at the start and didn't. If he brought this to their leader, he would want proof. Henry was stuck and had nowhere to turn. The only thing he could do now was hope he caught them, and that alone tore him up in some ways.

Knowing Jerry well, after over four years of living at the asylum together, Henry knew of his getaways. There was a place on the grounds where he liked to smoke weed when some came in from his hometown of Miami. He also had a place on the fourth floor where all the wheelchairs and extra beds and unused furniture was stored. There was only one floor above it, which had been converted to a lounge area in the half that wasn't destroyed by pests. But, the fourth floor was where Jerry liked to sneak off to be with his dirty magazines.

Henry came out of the stairway onto the fourth floor. He stepped lightly so his boots wouldn't echo down the hall on the hard tile floors. As he snaked through the discarded wheelchairs, just willy-nilly crammed in the hall, he heard commotion. At first, it was heavy breathing and grunts. It soon became screams and shouts of ecstasy.

At this point, it didn't matter who was in the room. They were breaking the laws of the colony. The community had strict understandings of their relationships. No sex. None. Not even masturbation.

Henry rounded the corner of an old restroom. It had three blue stalls, and only one of the doors was shut—the door hiding the scene producing all the noise. A couple tiles were cracked and flaked off the wall. The lights in the room dimmed and brightened without warning.

Kicking the door of the stall open, Henry saw what he feared. For some reason, he'd tricked himself into thinking that it may not be true. Almost like going crazy was better than having to incriminate his friend.

Rose, who had been leaning against the door while Jerry did his business, was knocked to the floor to the left of the toilet. She shrieked in pain and surprise. Her bottom lip was busted by the door smacking her in the mouth, and blood dribbled from the swollen gash.

To Henry, she was unimportant. Just another evil bag of bones that turned an otherwise good man into an animal. Whore.

Jerry stood there with his hands out, pleading with Henry to have pity. It was hard for Henry to see where he deserved any while his rock-hard member dripped Rose's juices from the end. He was no more than a demon to Henry now, and he must be punished for his unsavory ways.

"What a piece of shit you are," said Henry. It was all his mind could come up with. Everyone in the colony dealt with the pangs of abstinence, and this asshole thought he was more important or above living by the same set of rules.

"I'm sorry, man. I'm weak. I'm just a man who can't overcome the demons of carnal sin." Jerry wept into his hands.

Somewhere in the back of his mind, Henry knew he felt for his friend. Henry sneaked off every night to smoke a cigarette before bed. He would take deep drags and rub it out on the wall. When he finished, he'd bury them in the corner of the raised beds they grew beans in on the northwestern side of the grounds. If

Arthur caught wind of that, he'd have a conniption. He knew the struggle that came from avoiding your weakness. That wasn't something that didn't make a blip on his radar.

"Get up, now!" ordered Henry. He grabbed Jerry's jeans and shoved them in his chest. "Get dressed and come on."

"Henry, come on, man. You know I can't help it."

"Why not? You think you're the only one who wants to have sex? You think you're the only one who has had to sacrifice something they love for us to find our greater existence? What a selfish son of a bitch."

"Mr. Henry—"

"Shut up, whore," Henry snapped, cutting Rose off. "Close your mouth and learn how to close your legs."

"Don't talk to her like that, man," said Jerry.

Henry's mouth fell open in shock. He couldn't believe the words his friend said. How could Jerry possibly get an attitude with Henry in a time like this? He was in enough shit without also fighting for Rose to not be talked to in a certain way. It was an obvious slap in the face and disrespect for the lifestyle they agreed to live as brothers under Arthur guidance.

"Come on. Don't worry about the slash. She's less important than the soil they plant our crops in."

"This isn't right!" protested Jerry. "She's a person just like us. Just because she's a female everyone acts like she is a cockroach."

"She is a servant to a superior gender. She should be grateful for the chance, and you should've stayed the hell away from her and let her fulfill her highest potential. Instead, you decided to let her disgrace your honor and temple."

"You're spouting off the same shit as the old man. Open your eyes and mind. She's a person."

"She's going to be an example. Just like you."

"Mr. Henry—" Rose tried again.

Henry spun around on the ball of his foot and punched Rose in the mouth. Her teeth broke where his knuckles pounded into her face. The skin of her bottom lip split wider, and a geyser of fresh blood shot from the wound. Henry shook his hand where the woman's jagged, broken teeth busted his knuckles. The cuts in his hand stung from the bloody saliva in them.

Jerry jumped away from the violence. Rose fell to the floor, clutching her face and whimpering.

"What the fuck is wrong with you?" yelled Jerry, with one leg in his pants.

"I said come on. I'm not going to say it again."

"I'm trying t—"

Jerry suffered the same punch Rose did. There wasn't as much damage to his face as the lady's, but it rocked him, making stars swim in his vision. He stumbled backward, having to put a steadying hand down to keep from falling.

"What tha hell?" said Jerry through a hand covering his mouth. His voice was muffled by it, and blood leaked from his mouth around his meaty bandage.

"I told you, I'm not going to continue repeating myself. Every time you try to resist, that's going to happen."

Jerry mumbled and complained under his breath but followed Henry. Rose knew better than to say anything, and definitely didn't fight back.

They reached a large metal door on the first floor. A cheap, metal bracket for a name placard sat empty on its front. A fake, dusty plant in a woven, wicker basket decorated the left side of the door.

Henry rapped the door with his knuckles, then sucked air. "Damn, that hurts," he said. He through a sidelong, displeased glance at Jerry and Rose.

Footsteps behind the door warned them the

occupant was coming. The door swung open, and an older man, standing about five and a half feet tall and wearing thick glasses, stood before them. He looked surprised, almost happy to have company.

"What can I help you with, Henry?"

"Father Arthur, I found these two engaging in *the* sin." Henry pointed at the pair of offenders.

Arthur appraised the two. Rose refused to look him in the eye, although he lingered on her to tempt her. Jerry looked at a spot on the wall behind his right ear. It gave the illusion of looking at his leader without having to actually do so.

"Where?"

"They were on the fourth floor, in a bathroom. I've noticed them missing around this time for the last week or so."

"Why are they bloodied?" Arthur turned away and went into his study.

Henry and the other two followed.

"Because he hit us!" cried Jerry. Blood poured from his mouth when he removed his hand to speak.

"I didn't ask you," said Arthur. Violence bubbled beneath the voice. It was calm and serene, like a pot of water about to go into a roaring boil. "Did you really hit them?"

Henry dipped his head and shuffled his

feet. After stalling as long as he could, he answered, "Yes, Father."

Arthur slid a pair of latex gloves from a cardboard box and worked his wrinkled hands into them. He approached Jerry and moved his hand to check his wound.

Jerry winced a couple times as Arthur mashed and rubbed his busted lip and gums. When Arthur pulled a jar of petroleum jelly from his shelf and popped off the lid, Jerry's nostrils flared in fear.

Pulling a gob of product from the container on his forefinger, Arthur smeared it on Jerry's lip. Jerry recoiled from the man's touch. Arthur seemed offended by the action.

"Oh, what's this? Not only do you not trust my guidance with your everlasting soul, but now I'm not good enough to take care of your injuries." Arthur raised his eyebrows and nodded. "I see where your confidence in me stands."

"No, Father. I don't doubt your ability. I trust you with my all. I wouldn't have given up everything I worked my entire life for if I didn't. The problem is that it's sore to the touch. I'm sure that won't feel too good."

"You throw your sacrifice in my face, like it was forced upon you."

Arthur eased his hand to the man's face as he spoke. Jerry gritted his teeth and braved himself for the doctor's style of care.

"It was a choice. A choice you knew was important."

He smeared the jelly on Jerry's busted lip and added pressure in intervals. Soon, Jerry's eyes bulged and watered from the pain while the doctor pinched it between his thumb and forefinger, like he wanted to mash the wound back together. Tiny squeaks and whimpers escaped from Jerry's mangled and tortured lips.

"And now, we find ourselves in this position. Why would you commit the one sin that is seen so condemnable if you trust and believe in me and our mission on this earth so strongly? The actions are quite counterproductive to backing up your words, aren't they?"

Jerry's face was as red as the blood pouring from his mouth. Without noticing, he'd held his breath. He was staring forward, but his eyes were vacant, like he had left the world, mentally. He held on as long as he could, then he passed out. From the pain or not breathing, either way, it ended in the same result.

Arthur seemed amused. The corners of his mouth tugged upwards ever-so-slightly, and rosiness blossomed in his cheeks. He turned around and went to sit behind the steel and clouded glass desk in the back of the room beside the hallway leading to the rest of the suite.

"What about Rose?" said Henry.

Arthur looked up, first at him, then to her. "Oh, gosh. I forgot about the cunt." Leave her here. I'll take care of her removal from the community."

"Wait!" shouted Rose. "Wait a minute. I'm sorry. I can make it up to you, Father Arthur. I can't help Jerry's weakness, but I can still my own resolve. I can take a vow of silence, and also a new vow of abstinence and servitude."

"Tsk tsk." Arthur shook his head. "Do you see this, Henry? Do you see how the unknowing and weak gender of our race will throw us males under the bus at the first sign of trouble?"

Henry nodded; eyes big.

"This shows you why they are not to be trusted. And, all women are this way. A true, strong person is willing to stand by someone they love, regardless of the sacrifices. Women are weak by nature. It crosses over from the physical aspects to the mental. She just showed you firsthand."

Henry looked at Rose like she was a science project. Somewhere in his eyes, terror danced. There was a part of him that felt as though the woman was a demon in human form.

And, that's exactly how Arthur wanted it.

When Jerry came to, he was in a room he had no recollection of. White walls were stained with brown streaks, burnt orange encapsulating them. The streaks dwindled in size the closer to the floor they ran. Corroded pipes ran along the ceiling where the thickest part of the rusty residue was. There was a long window with metal cross work reinforcing it between two panes of glass. It was situated on the same wall as the door, and there was a cream, canvas curtain covering it.

He was restrained to the aluminum rails of an ancient hospital bed. A blue, rubber mattress peeled his skin when he moved. It grabbed and shrieked when he adjusted his naked body, and his flesh stung like a thousand bees attacked him. Rattling from the bed's frame echoed off the cinder block walls. At one point, Jerry was concerned over whether or not the bed could hold him.

His lips felt like his heartbeat began there. They pounded and throbbed. When Jerry tried to yell, his lips vibrated and made him feel queasy. He, instead, mumbled as tears came to his eyes.

A steel table sat beside him. Various tools and implements were placed neatly on its surface. A lot of things that they could be used for crossed his mind, and none of them excited him. The fluorescent lights glistened on the scalpels, scissors, and needles, giving them an angelic facade.

The gray door swung open. Black hand-smudges framed the metal handle. A cold blast of air rushed into the stuffy, little room. The dull rumble of something heavy on wheels filled Jerry's ears.

Arthur pushed a four-foot-tall box with a silver face, a few random knobs, and a line of lights. On the right side was a handle with two probes and a coiled wire ran from the box to it.

The door snapped shut behind him. The weight of the door was apparent. All the air in the room felt sucked out of Jerry's mouth, nose, and ears.

The doctor came into Jerry's view leaning on the heavy, blue machine to catch his breath. Arthur hung his head, chest rising and dropping with each deep heave.

"Those damn stairs are hard to get down with this thing." He wiped his forehead with the back of his hand. "I need to find a place to keep it down here, so I don't have to work so hard to do my teachings."

"What are you doing, Father?" moaned Jerry. His lips hurt with each syllable spoken.

"Oh! Yes, I should tell you what's going on." Arthur nodded in agreement. "I am … reaffirming your faith."

"You mean you're not going to banish me?"

"Don't be a fool, my son." He patted Jerry's shoulder. "I am forgiving, just like our lord and savior. I wouldn't dare destroy a man's chance at finding their salvation, regardless of their transgressions and how far, or near, in the past they occurred. That's not what I've been given this life for."

Comfort settled over Jerry. He didn't understand what all the restraints and ceremony was about, but he felt better about where things were heading.

"Thank you, Father. I'm sorry about my mistake. My sin was egregious, and I know it. You are a great man, and great prophet, for forgiving me."

Arthur didn't speak. He uncurled a cord from the back of the blue box and plugged it into an outlet in the wall. A dull hum issued from inside the box, and the boards lit up red.

"What would you say you felt the most remorseful about?" Arthur said. His face was as inquisitive as his tone. He rested his chin on his fist, arm braced on his chest. The man's brow furrowed as he listened with such intent it was visible.

"I'm not sure. I feel bad about my weakness. I wish I could stop myself, but it's such a hard thing to do. It was the thing I hated giving up the most when I joined." Jerry realized he'd never said that out loud. Something in the statement was astounding in its freedom. He felt lighter, like a weight had been lifted from his chest and shoulders.

"I think I can help with that," said Arthur. "I'm glad you said what you did. I truly feel like you wish you were different, rather than the situation."

"What do you mean?"

"Meaning, I feel like you're not just upset you got caught. That's a good thing. We can strengthen weaknesses and fix things that need work. Changing a selfish thought process and pattern of behavior is far harder to alter."

Jerry nodded. "I understand, and it's true. I'm not upset about getting busted. I'm even grateful that I was. It gives me a chance, and by your forgiving hands, to reform."

"You are a beautiful soul, my son." Arthur smiled and rubbed the follower's bicep. "My god and I are lucky to have such a loyal and loving soldier."

Arthur took the handle with the two circle, metal probes from the blue machine. Jerry noticed how much it looked like an old rotary phone receiver with the probes sticking out from the earpiece.

When Arthur turned one the knobs to the right, the droning noise grew louder. The unmistakable buzz of electrical current made the anxiety in Jerry's core rise rapidly.

"What are you doing?" said Jerry, jerking and pulling his hands and feet. The bed moaned and creaked beneath him, but neither the rails nor the shackles gave in to his protests in the slightest.

"What do you mean? We just talked about what I'm doing. We both agreed: you need to be fixed."

In the doctor's eyes was a crazed look. A mad, frantic mania blossomed inside him. It was something Jerry associated with serial killers and psychopaths, like Charles Manson.

A distant smile crossed Arthur's lips. He was in there somewhere, but someone else had taken over the little man's body. There was no way he was the same person Jerry trusted and gave his servitude to.

"How are you going to do that?" Jerry yelled. Panic was setting deep inside him.

"Stay still!" snapped Arthur.

He pressed the two metal probes on either side of Jerry's testicles. The cold probes slid into place like the gap between them was made perfect for his balls.

Arthur turned a wing nut-like thing on the handle the probes met on. The grip on Jerry's nuts tightened with each crank. The pressure grew uncomfortable, and his scrotum plumped up and turned a violent shade of red. The veins in his sack became pronounced and darker by the second.

"Father," breathed Jerry.

Arthur answered by punching him in his swollen, mangled mouth. Jerry bucked and cried. His whimpering trailed off to quiet sobs.

"You want me to fix you. Now, you have to let me do it. No one said it would be easy. True remorse is achieved with pain." Arthur rubbed his knuckles after the strike. Sharp pain shot through his hand.

The doctor turned a knob on the far right of the silver face. The blue machine began to vibrate and click.

"Calm down, Blue Belle." Arthur rubbed the machine on top like he consoled it. "Get warmed up. It's time to work."

After a few moments, the whirring and moaning subsided, and Arthur smiled. The red lights changed to green across the board. He turned another dial, creeping it up ever so slowly.

The noise ascended again. A quiet knocking accompanied the electric clicking. And then came the screams.

Jerry lost his mind. He shouted so loud his voice cracked, and the lungs in his chest were empty sacks of flesh.

Electrical current coursed through his genitals. He felt each volt flow into the nerves in his sack and spark to life at the ends of his ungroomed pubic hair. His penis was a lightning rod, although it was flaccid. His back arched, and he contorted. His jaw clinched. The pressure was so great, he was concerned he would break his teeth.

"Just a little more," Arthur shouted over the electrical noise and Jerry's grunts of pain.

Sparks popped from the pores on Jerry's scrotum. His hair began falling off. The insides of his thighs ached. His blood thickened from the intensity, and his muscles became weaker.

As Arthur lessened the current being forced into Jerry's body, Jerry's feet slid, and he relaxed. His breathing was still labored and sweat poured from him. Tiny puddles of moisture collected on the rubber mattress.

Arthur noticed a tear spilling from Jerry's eyes. "Oh, my son," he said, "is it too much to bear?"

Jerry nodded, and his lip quivered like he'd been in a blizzard.

"It hurt me just this much to find out about your indiscretions. Probably more."

"I'm sorry," croaked Jerry. He couldn't believe he was saying the words, but he meant them. He wasn't sorry in the way Arthur took it in his narcissistic, insanity-laden mind. He was saying it about what he was going through. For that, he was truly sorry.

"I know you are, but I don't think it's sunk

in yet," said Arthur. He licked his lips and jacked the knob up again.

Jerry went rigid. Goosebumps erupted under his thick, black body hair. His mouth clamped so hard, his jaw came loose from it socket. His eyes squeezed until the blood vessels inside them popped, and tears of blood trickled from his eyes. An arch of golden piss shot high into the air and landed on his chest with a sickening splatter.

"You have all the impulse control of a three-year-old." Arthur shook his head. "You're such an embarrassment."

If Jerry heard a word the doctor said, he didn't give a shit. There wasn't even the slightest acknowledgment.

Arthur, however, took the offender's writhing as a signal to raise the intensity.

"We're getting closer, I think. The message seems to be setting in as deeply as I would've hoped," Arthur yelled over all the ruckus. The noise got to him after a while, so he held his hands over his ears.

Smoke rose from Jerry's genitals, and the capillaries began breaking under his skin. Tiny bruises and purple splotches pock-marked him. Glowing electrical current pulsed through his veins.

Arthur backed the juice off with the exuberance a dead man could muster.

Jerry's body wilted as the voltage lessened. Deep heaves of relief replaced frantic breaths and accompanied high-pitched whimpers. He pushed through the pain.

"I'm sorry, Father," Jerry said. His dried, cracked throat made his voice less than a peep.

Arthur chuckled. His cheeks turned red, like the tale of Santa Claus. "Oh, my boy, I know you are! If I never believed it from anyone before, I believe it from you."

Jerry tried to look at the doctor because his voice seemed to have come from his right when he remembered the opposite. When his eyelids started parting, it felt like he ripped the skin apart. He couldn't do it. He'd been through enough already.

"What's the matter, my boy? Can't you feel that?" Arthur said.

Jerry shook his head. He didn't know what the doctor was talking about, nor did he really give a damn, as long as it didn't hurt, and it was almost over.

"Are you sure? I need you to really focus and tell me."

If he wasn't so traumatized, Jerry would've asked what the doctor was talking about, or why he stood at his feet. But whatever got him closer to being unchained to the bed and let go from Arthur's crazy playground he would do. He shook his head again.

"Ah, perfect then." Arthur rubbed his hands together.

"My dick doesn't work anymore. Even arousing thoughts hurt my balls. When I pee, it dribbles out. I can't stop it in public. It's embarrassing." Jerry stared Henry in the eyes. Anger sparkled over his entire body like road flares just coming to life. It didn't matter to him. He wanted to kill his former friend. A couple of tough words were nothing.

"You act like this is my fault," Henry said. "I wasn't the one pounding away on some garden slut and hiding it for weeks, maybe longer. You had a chance to quit. I searched for you two and couldn't find you. You should've taken your opportunity."

"Fuck you, asshole. Did you not hear me? My shit is broken. He electrocuted me until I couldn't use anything. And your reply, the man who busted me, isn't a consoling comment, an apology, asking do I know where Rose went off to. None of that shit crossed your mind. All you wanted to do was blame me."

"Your childish and foul words do nothing but prove your immaturity. It shows how much you have left to grow. I'm saddened by my friend's inability to accept the gift that's been given to you."

"Gift? You can't be serious?"

"How do you see it any other way?"

"You better hope you see death the same

way as you do this idiotic gift you're talking about because I'm about to kill you."

"You need to calm down. You've been through plenty. You don't need to add an ass whipping to it."

"Whoa, boys. What's the problem here?" Conner Crowe stepped between Jerry and Henry.

Thick drapes of dark hair framed his face. A beaked nose angled his appearance forward jutting past his wavy curtains like his squared jaw. A t-shirt covered his chiseled stomach, and the flannel shirt over it bulked up his shoulders. His hands came from the pockets of his faded blue jeans and put them out to stop the men.

"This isn't your business, sir," said Henry. "Let me handle this, please. It's personal."

"I can tell," Conner's voice was warm but was laced with threats of violence. "Judging by the way things were going, though, you were failing in doing so."

Henry went to speak but was cut off by Jerry.

"You can go to hell, too. I don't give a shit what any of you think. I've been damaged for life."

"And you should thank Father Arthur for making your weakness impossible to indulge in. He saved you, and you're too damn selfish to realize it," said Conner.

"I'm not selfish. I'm a goddamn victim!" Jerry's self-control had dwindled down to almost nothing. He was one flippant reply from losing his last drop of sanity.

Conner grabbed Jerry's shoulder and slammed him into the cement wall. Conner's firm, hairy forearm pressed beneath his chin. Jerry's air flow was restricted, and his feet dangled no more than three inches from the floor.

Jerry grabbed and clawed at the man choking him out. In some sick way, Jerry hoped Conner would kill him. It would be a mercy killing.

"You will watch your worthless mouth, or I'll beat it 'til it's swollen shut. The only thing you should open it for is to let a dick inside. You are nothing. I don't know who told you that you have even *one* right to speak to your superiors in such a way, but it's going to leave you ending up in a lake or ditch, or something." He let go of Jerry.

Jerry's feet touched the ground, and he sucked in a huge, cool shot of air, grasping at his neck and coughing. It burned his lungs and throat. A rumble escaped his esophagus, and he winced from the pain.

While Jerry was bent double, Conner was still as a statue. He wasn't going to let the disrespectful shit by before apologizing.

"Answer me, little man. I'm giving you as much opportunity as I can before you get on my bad side."

"Fuck your bad side." The sputtering subsided enough for Jerry's voice to be closer to normal, but it hurt him to do so. Everyone around them stopped moving and waited to see what came next.

"No. Fuck your life," said Conner, and punched Jerry in the temple.

Jerry fell to the ground with a hard, lifeless thud. The crown of his head slammed the concrete hard enough his hair jolted. It made Henry nauseous.

"Leave him alone, man. He's gone through enough, don't you think?" Henry pushed Conner back before he even realized what he'd done.

For his trouble, and momentary lapse of judgment, Conner punched him in the jaw. The bone dislodged from its socket, and his chin sunk on the side he was struck on. Henry did a half spin, took a stuttered step, and fell to his knees.

"Got anything else to say?" It was clear Conner wasn't expecting an answer.

Behind them, a small crowd had formed. Ben, Nick, Brandon, and Dave stood there with mouths agape and a look of terror on their faces. Sally and Theresa were further down the hall in their kitchen maid uniforms, but their eyes were glued to the action just like the men were.

"Conner, stop it," Arthur said, walking into the corridor from a door leading to the stairs. "I believe your point's been made ... a couple times, in fact."

Behind Arthur, Cameron came running looking like a bantam rooster with a smug look on his face and his chest bowed out. He was five-feet tall, when he wore his boots, and maybe broke one-hundred and twenty pounds in the middle of his heaviest winter cushioning. He grew a beard, but it grew in thin patches and had wispy, adolescent hairs. Everybody hated him, and even the women disrespected him. However, he was Arthur's tattle tale, and although he hated and mistreated him too, he used him for the dirt he brought him on the members of the community.

"Yes, sir," said Conner through gritted teeth. He saw Cameron bouncing behind Arthur like an over-excited Jack Russell Terrier and was ready to kill the little son of a bitch. "They were disrespecting you."

Arthur nodded. "I'm sure. That seems to be an affliction that's going around. It needs to be addressed but not with barbarism. There's a better way."

"I'm sorry, Father Arthur. It gets me hot when someone runs you down, after all you've given to us."

"I know. It's okay." Arthur patted the man's back. "Pick that one up, the one that hasn't moved since I got here. This one can walk. It's just his jaw that's broken. Not his leg."

The mood in the dinner hall was more subdued than a funeral. Everyone knew things were a little out of hand among parts of the community, and they were going to be addressed and discussed. Word had spread all over the group after the altercation between the boys in the hall. No one was foolish enough to believe it was going to be passed over.

Arthur came into the room, and the chattering went silent. You could hear people breathe. The air flowing in and out of the doors of the hall seemed to have its own voice. A dull hum, with an underlying shriek.

He looked around at all the people hovering over their dinner trays. Some had cream colored, sectioned school lunch trays. A couple of royal blue and stop-sign-red ones broke the monogamy. Baked chicken breasts, boiled carrots, cucumbers and vinegar, unusually vibrant green beans, and three-by-three-inch squares of cornbread dressed all the trays. The fear and anxiety exuding from every last one of them exhilarated the doctor.

When Arthur slid his tray down the buffet line, he noticed the kitchen lady's reluctance to make eye contact. It was typical for them not to speak unless he invited them to, but they would look at him, hoping for the acknowledgment.

It was important to Arthur to not show his

happiness, though. He didn't want anyone to think the type of behavior going on among the members as of late would be taken lightly. He had to put off the vibe that he was beyond pissed off. The energy coming from him must be intense, strong enough people around him must feel dwarfed by his presence.

The doctor sat down at his normal spot. A table closest to the food line, with only one chair tucked under it. A hard, composite seat and back chair, with a shiny, steel bar frame.

To the left of Arthur's table was the emergency exit. It looked like it was in the back of the room, but in reality, he sat in the one place that allowed him to see everyone in the dining hall and be the first out in case there was a need for a quick evacuation.

Tables of four to six people waited to hear what Arthur said. No one even pretended to eat. They stared into their leader's wide-open eyes, knowing his mouth would be soon to follow.

"Eat first," he barked. "I need to collect myself." He sounded gruff and short. That made him proud.

All the people in the dinner hall began shuffling their food about their trays. None of them looked to be hungry. A few ate, but it was slow, like they were testing their stomachs after a virus or something. The tentativeness of eating wore off after about five minutes. No one was enthusiastic about dinner, however. Downcast gazes and shifty eyes were the norm for this meal.

Twenty-five minutes or so later, Arthur stood from the table. He placed his dinner tray in the conveyor line and shoved the last bite of cornbread into his mouth. The sweet sponge dried his mouth out. He coughed a couple times while he filled his clear plastic cup with water from the pitcher on the buffet. The ice-cold water forced down the flaky bread before choking to death became a legitimate concern.

When he spun to face the dinner hall, Arthur saw every person's eyes on him. It was like he was Jesus walking on water, or something just as spectacular. That feeling never got old to him.

"Well, you all know what has been going on here," Arthur began. Half the crowd held their breaths. From experience, he knew that showed guilt, so he made a mental note of the ones who gave their silent confession without consent. "Members of our loving and enlightened little group are backsliding from the teachings and common core goals we seek to achieve.

"Our lives here are not easy, nor are they made to be. We see the truth the rest of humanity is blind to. It is why we have separated ourselves from them. When the time comes for us to be called forward to speak to our lord, we will be the pure and worthy. He has told me this is true.

"I care enough about you all to put you on the correct path laid out to me by God. I have not read this from a book. I have not interpreted it from words another man wrote. I have not taken classes and had another man tell me what to say with theatrics coupled with perfectly timed shouts and over-the-top deliveries.

"I have been told by our lord. Why would you question his word? Why would you question *my* word?"

The people who held their breaths, looked at the ground, and at the walls, or ceiling, or anywhere but at the doctor. Their guilt became ever clearer to him. He could taste it, like the fat and sugar-enriched cheap butter substitute spread on the top of the cornbread that almost killed him.

The most devout stared at him. Some nodded in their agreement. Arthur liked them. They followed without asking questions. They trusted his words. He returned their love because they gave his words power.

But, it was true. They're all sinners. Most people there were working on their faith in Arthur and his demands for the perfect soul.

"Everyone here needs constant love, hope, support ... and work. I don't expect you to be perfect all the time. God has conversed with me. I am the exception. I worked my whole life to reach this level of purity and perfection. I had to make God trust me. And, he finally did.

"I am not God. I am a normal man, humble and mortal. I have only been given a light and love, by our lord, and a narrative to the story of our lives.

"This is no secret, however. Each of you knew this when you joined. We discussed and agreed on these facts when you came to live at the community. So, why are some of you fighting back on this, now?"

"I would never fight your word, Father," Byron, one of the local converts, cried out.

Arthur held his hand up and nodded. "I know, my boy, I know. Most of you are unwavering in your faith and journey toward your own salvation." He dropped his head for a moment, just enough to build anticipation. "But a few ... a few of you have really bucked against the community."

He took a couple steps toward the crowd. "Those of you who feel above this knot of like-souled individuals will leave this community at once. We have already lost a few members in the last couple days. Sister Rose and Brother Jerry have committed the unforgivable sin. We all know what it is, I don't need to elaborate on their filthy weakness. They have since been removed from the group.

"It is sad when we lose any number of our family. We are nothing if one tooth of our cog wheel is broken. We must rise above pull together stronger, hunker down, and push forward as one cohesive unit. Love your brothers. Sisters, serve your brothers, so they can be the strongest men that our lord has ever created."

Conner stood. "I have shown I will fight for your honor and respect. I'm not scared to fight more. Physically, mentally, or emotionally."

"That's where you missed the message," said Arthur, shaking his head. "I don't want us to fight. I want us to love."

A relieved exhale of a hundred and fifty people filled the air in the room. The surprising happy energy of the crowd unnerved and pissed off Arthur.

"Make no mistake, though," he cut across the forming smiles on the faces looking at him, "refusing to adhere to the rules and teachings of this family will lead to banishment. No questions. No discussion. No mercy."

His last two words rang with menacing undertones in Steve's ears.

II

Steve knew things would have to end at some point. The fear of losing everything that had grown between he and Angie almost made him physically ill, even when it was understood from the start there couldn't be a real future. Over time, the loose rule they made became foolish to follow.

The matter felt quite pressing after the speech in the dinner hall. Arthur made it plain things were tightening up in the community. Sins and backsliding would be persecuted to the highest degree. There was no room for mistakes.

When he reached his room, he took off his button-down shirt, and hung it on the bed post of the twin bed that looked just like the ones all the members slept in. He pulled his dog tags over his head and laid them on the composite wood dresser that matched the bed furniture.

Exhaling as he collapsed on the bed, Steve's mind raced. Was the world he lived in really worth giving up Angie? Blue, prison-style comforters, cheap ass decor, shared restrooms and showers, and cramped living arrangements. Plus, there was the ever-present possibility that Arthur may crank down on the lifestyle they'd come accustomed to.

On the other side of that, Steve had an extreme faith in the life he led. He gave up his wife—who refused to come along with him for a life of servitude—his kids, and his property. He never thought twice when his wife's lawyer asked him to sign on the dotted line for divorce—giving her the house, his motorcycle, complete custody of the children, his one year old, fully-loaded Mercedes-Benz, and half of his life savings, which came up to just short three-hundred-thousand dollars. Other than travel to meet with the community and move to the compound, Arthur got the other half.

Steve never questioned his decision on giving all of those things away. Not even his kids. His wife and sister let it be known how much of a lowlife asshole they thought he was for leaving his own flesh and blood so willingly, but he saw it differently. It was the ultimate sacrifice. The greatest offering he could give his lord and best gift he could give to his kids. Changing the world through his actions may open their eyes when they came of age.

Sadly, things didn't work out that way. Billy and Emma felt abandoned by him when he walked out in 1992. He moved away without so much as a phone call on Christmas. He did send birthday cards and letters regularly, but his ex-wife claimed to never receive them, which he thought was utter bullshit.

Instead, by the time both the boy and girl turned eighteen, he'd lost track of their whereabouts altogether. Letter after letter went unanswered, where he begged them to join him in the holy land of Green's Bay, Africa. He guessed, after five years of trying, they wrote him off dead, or just as well in their opinion.

Africa was his home. He knew it the minute he landed on the continent. The ride to Green's Bay, the gated community they occupied, was wondrous. Steve never forgot how he couldn't breathe on the bouncy bus trip. Excitement ran through him like electrical current through a power line. So, even if he decided against staying, he doubted he'd go back to his home in Boston.

The fact that he was caught between his soul or a woman made him think on a deeper level. The biggest sin in the community was sex. It was looked down on in all regards. Feelings harbored for someone who you committed the terrible act with would be akin to a Christian giving the devil a handjob. Steve didn't know if there was a death penalty or an exorcism for such an occasion, but he was reluctant to find out.

He needed to talk to Angie about what to

do. She had just as much say in their next move as he did. In reality, he was likely to listen to her opinion over his own. He cared a lot about her, her comfort, and her happiness, but he would have to wait until their normal meeting time to discuss it with her.

During Arthur's address of the community, the two had made sure to not even acknowledge the other's existence. They did that all the time among the general population. Sometimes Steve found it quite hard to tear his eyes from her wonderful, flaring hips. The way they swished back and forth as she mopped the floors, and her plump butt sticking up when she pulled weeds from the raised bed gardens on the grounds.

One thing that tempted him to leave, which was petty and dumb—but still a temptation, was seeing her hair. The rule for females in Green's Bay was for them to keep it cut above their shoulder blades. Any style was allowed as long as it stayed short. And when they were anywhere, other than the Spring and Fall Solstice Balls, it was to be tied up. Steve had always wanted her to grow it down to the middle of her back. She said if they left the community, she would love to. She missed the long, blonde strands of her thick mane.

Steve pressed his toe to his heel and kicked his shoes off. He grabbed the book he'd been reading on self-enlightenment, penned by none other than Arthur Green—their all-knowing leader—and lay back in bed. In two days, he would learn of his future. Until then, he had to act as normal as possible. With Arthur's last words, n*o mercy,* and the penetrating look the doctor threw at him during his speech, that would be stressful. He and Angie had gotten by with their side business for over two years, though. Two days shouldn't be too hard.

Things in the community were better, as far as people getting busted for sins and indiscretions. Arthur smiled and hugged his brothers and bounced when he walked, like he did before the darkness came to light. Dinners and breakfasts went by smoother.

Like the underbelly of sinning was hidden from Arthur, so, too, was the newly imposed tension. Although it plagued the members of the Green's Bay Community, the rising boil had not yet come to a roll. Everyone, even the quiet, mousy women, felt things growing too volatile to control.

One night in the showers, Conner and Ralph had a tense interaction. Steve thought Conner may have finally met his match, and Ralph, a three-hundred seventeen-pound former Hell's Angel, had no intentions of stepping down. It took five men to keep Ralph off Conner once he shoved him down. Some of the say-but-don't-do guys claimed it only took that many guys to hold Ralph back because the floor was wet, and they were sliding—a point in which Steve debunked by saying it only took one to *talk* Conner out of the fight, and the conditions were just as slippery for everyone involved.

That was the most obvious of several moments of overflowing frustration. A few snappy replies, a couple sights of shouldering between a few people, and even a screaming match or two.

Conner, Arthur's favorite little asshole, was at the center of most of the issues. That was a surprise to no one. It was quite expected by most, in fact.

The night Steve usually met with Angie had been bumped due to Conner's incessant beleaguering and obsessive bullshit. He had worked it up in his violent, fucked up mind that everyone at the community was hiding something Arthur needed to be made aware of. No one had seen him sleep in days.

To the surprise of most people there, Conner had been reprimanded by Arthur one morning at breakfast. It came in a coddling delivery, but Arthur still told him to chill out with all his ridiculous hounding of the other members.

"Conner, my boy," he'd said. "You need some rest. You haven't changed clothes, showered, or slept that I can tell in three days' time. Your devotion to this place is beyond what our lord could hope for in a soldier of his will, but you need to be healthy to enforce his word. Some of our brothers in faith need you to give them a rest, too."

Conner nodded and looked proud of himself. Everyone around him felt his sheer joy at being told he'd terrorized the whole community to the point they asked Arthur to tell him to stop. It was sickening to Steve.

Deep down, Steve only went through the motions of day to day life. He really looked forward to getting with Angie. The situation with her was a cause for a lot of his stress, but she was also the only person he felt comfortable unloading his grievances. Plus, seeing her face, her beauty, and easiness of her presence, made him soften. His life seemed a better one to live since meeting her.

Sometimes, Angie reminded him of his ex-wife. There were some physical things, like the way she parted her hair slightly to the right, the way she ate corn on the cob in little nibbles, or the way she'd swirl the head of his cock when she gave him a blow job. Those things took him back to married life, but there were others. The way it seemed their souls knew each other, the way they could look at each other and know what the other was thinking, the way she fit in the crease of his arm like an adjoining puzzle piece. He never missed his ex, but he did miss the affection and connection on a deeper level than a hug and a handshake.

Angie had her own reasons he loved her for, more so than his wife did, really. She didn't fuss and bitch at him every day about how hard her job was, how much she hated it, or the people she worked with. She kept herself clean, smelled like raspberries, and always smiled.

Her smile was what he'd first fell for. It shined through the dinner hall. All the women sat in the far-right corner of the room at the same table. The only reason they were to mingle with the men were if they were addressed or needed to serve one of the guys' needs. They were allowed to converse among each other. They weren't slaves.

One morning at breakfast, he'd asked the ladies' table to bring him some orange juice from the back. Angie was the one that answered the request.

She brought him the pitcher of juice and refilled his empty glass. She sat the glass on the table and asked did anyone else want some. The smile that could melt a million hearts, in Steve's opinion, backed her words up.

In that moment, Steve felt his insides flutter. He didn't think it was his heart or his dick. It was somewhere in the middle. Butterflies slammed into his soul and floated around his testicles like they were moths around a flood light. No matter what she had affected, he knew, at that moment, he was in trouble.

Over time, their communication became

more extensive. Steve was even warned by Conner a couple times, and Arthur once in the dinner hall for him sitting with her while they ate cake. After the incident with Arthur, they began meeting a couple times a week away from prying eyes. The location moved every two weeks. They recycled a couple meeting spots, because they enjoyed them so much.

The roof of the building on top of the smaller air conditioning units toward the north end was their favorite spot. On Saturdays, the two would get together around one or two in the morning and lie there, stargazing. It had become their most romantic date. Sometimes, Angie would sneak a couple extra desserts out from the kitchen (if she could) and bring for them to snack on. The way the blowers on the unit rose around them, hiding their bodies, and sending any noise they made into the heavens with the fan, made them feel safer there than any place on the grounds. They'd play wrestle, tickle fight, sing, and make the best love of their lives there. It was like a tiny island of affection.

Recently, Tuesdays had been at the loading door for the kitchen, and Saturdays were a third-floor room that seemed to be an old, abandoned isolation room. It was soundproof and had soft walls and floor. There was no bed, no furniture, nothing but dust and a dingy pile of strait jackets thrown into the corner. It didn't need anything more, except Steve and Angie.

The Tuesday date had to be skipped over, but the isolation room date was on without any hurdles.

Angie sat on the floor, leaning against the wall. Her arms wrapped around her knees that were curled up to her chest. Her silky hair brushed the exposed skin on her shoulders, which was a rarity, because the females were only allowed to wear t-shirts or something that covered more skin than that. Freckles accented her pale skin. It was one of Steve's favorite characteristics to point out to her.

As she traced an unfocused finger through the dust on the floor, her date hopped through the door. She jumped to her feet and dove on him, hanging from his neck and squeezing his waist with her legs. She kissed his face about ten times. It was cute.

There was an obvious blocking of the happiness by Steve. He wanted to talk, so there was a cold, hard divider.

"What's the problem? I thought you'd be as happy to see me as I am you. It's been longer than usual. I missed you."

"I missed you, too, but that's kind of the problem with what we need to talk about."

"I don't understand," she said, rubbing her

chin. "Has this got anything to do with the shit with Conner?"

"Pretty much. He's not really the concern, though. I'm more worried about what he represents. The pain and suffering and landmines in the way."

"Do you want to stop seeing each other?"

Steve shook his head. "Not at all, but I want you to feel free to do so if you'd like. I've also thought about leaving the community, if you'd like. I just want you to know I'm here for you and support anything you decide."

"I have never questioned you or your love for me, Steve. It's not just my choice, though." She rubbed his smooth face where his sideburns would be, if they were allowed. "This is a two-way street, and always has been."

"I know that, but my happiness is predicated on being with you. Honestly, that's something I wasn't sure about until I felt you. I had logic dictate every thought about this situation up until the minute you touched me. Everything after that seems secondary."

"That's sweet, but I think we need this place," said Angie. "It brought us together. It's how we met and fell in love. Maybe, in time, Arthur will soften on the relationship thing, and if not, that doesn't change anything for us. We can always change our minds and leave any time we like."

"I doubt Arthur will change his feelings. I've been here around twenty-five years, and that point has only been enforced stronger in that time. I've seen many men and women shuffle in and out because of that, and many other reasons. Rose and Jerry are far from the first. But if you want to wait for him to magically welcome marriage and gender equality, then you're going to be heartbroken."

"And, again, we can leave whenever we see fit. Those two did. So can we."

"If you're sure, I'm sure. I'm glad to stand behind anything you want, as long as my arms are wrapped around you."

"You're the most amazing man. No wonder you traveled across the globe to find your true potential. I am lucky to call you mine. Arthur is lucky to call you a brother. I love you. And our lord must be proud to call you his child."

The sweet moment led to heavy kissing and passionate sex. Both had monstrous orgasms and collapsed in a panting heap on the floor. Steve held his love until she told him they needed to head back to their bunks. He agreed, but his dozing mind was cloudy. He needed her.

At dinner, a little more than two months later, Angie delivered water to the table Steve, Jones, and Brandon ate at. Jones had requested it, so it didn't come off as suspicious. When she dropped a piece of napkin into Steve's lap as she turned away to the kitchen, things changed.

Steve didn't immediately react to the situation. He played it cool, realizing no one else around him caught on to her act, but if he jumped out at the little piece of paper, they'd call attention to their exchange.

In a few moments time, Steve dropped his dinner knife on the ground. It clattered around, and he grunted: all the typical things someone would do in that instance. No one even paid attention, so Steve scooped up the fragment of napkin in the same motion he did the knife.

Sitting up in his chair and putting his knife on the table, Steve made sure there were no eyes on him as he unfolded the paper. In all capital red lettering, it read: EMERGENCY MEETING. ROOFTOP @ 10.

Steve reeled for a split second. In over three years, this was the first time this had happened. They had discussed it in case it ever came up. They worked through the plan hundreds of times, but things and tension had calmed down so much in the last couple months. Conner no longer tried to create reasons to beat his brother's asses. Jerry, Henry, and Rose had left the community. What could be the problem?

It didn't matter what it was at the moment. In fact, on par with how their entire relationship had gone, Angie acted as though Steve didn't exist the rest of their time in the dinner hall. That would have made Steve proud, under normal circumstances, but this pissed him off and shook him.

Jones clapped Steve on the back when they walked away from the tray belt. Steve jumped and yelped like a dog shot with an arrow.

"Whoa, boy!" Jones jerked away from Steve. "What's the matter with you?"

"Oh, God," said Steve, gasping for air. "I don't know why, but you just scared me out of my skin." He clutched his chest.

"I'm sorry, brother," said the big, native man. His voice was deep and strong. Booming. Intimidating, yet comforting, much like his presence as a whole. "I didn't mean to startle you."

Steve shook his head. "It's not your fault. Just caught me off guard."

"Looks like someone is carrying more burden than they can handle," said Arthur, who had crept up behind them. "Only time someone finds themselves that easily frightened is when they aren't living right."

Steve and Jones turned around to see him say the last bit. He ended with a smile and wink.

"I've been eating too much bread. Put on five pounds in the last two months," Steve laughed.

"Gluttony is a sin, my boy, but not worthy of condemnation." Arthur winked again and turned down the hall heading to the east side of the building, where his own room was.

Both Steve and Jones waited a moment before speaking again. Something about the way Arthur appeared got to them a little bit. He seemed to just materialize behind them as they talked, but that was silly. The dining hall was open. They ran into Arthur all the time. It was just this time that freaked them out. Maybe it was the fear settling from Steve's overreaction.

On the way to their rooms, Jones and Steve talked about the usual bullshit. They had a few laughs over how shitty and dry the polenta was and how they miss ice cream. Lime Jell-O just didn't cut it anymore. They reminisced over some of the meals Lani used to cooked before she left the community because she stood up to Arthur one day about being talked down to. The woman may have been crazy, but she was one hell of a cook. They missed her.

Steve did his normal stuff: taking off his shirt, and his jewelry, and then climbing into bed with his book. It was nightly. He enjoyed this routine. He felt like he grew smarter and more stable every day because of it. There wasn't hours of weightlifting and exercise. It was just him and a book, resting and learning. It made him happier and calmer.

Although he had a hard time getting into a reading rhythm, soon the clock was at 9:57. He felt like it took three days for the three hours to pass by from dinner until the time to meet Angie. It came, but it was slow.

Hopping out of bed and throwing on the shirt he hung from his bed post when he got in from dinner, Steve zoomed out of his room and down the hall to the stairs. He went right up to the roof without hesitation.

As he came out of the door into the night air, Steve expected his normal welcome hug, but instead he was greeted by tears and sobs. Angie was a complete mess, and it scared the hell out of him.

"Calm down, honey. Tell me what's wrong, please," said Steve. She got more upset. "Hey. Hey! Just breathe."

He grabbed her hands and breathed alongside her, until she calmed down. Steve had never seen her like this and couldn't fathom what the problem was.

"Can you talk now?" he said.

She nodded, sniffled, and wiped her eyes. "I'm sorry," she squeaked. "I'm so upset and don't know what to do."

"What's the problem?"

"I'm pregnant."

Days went by, weeks, with the same routine. Breakfast, work, dinner, shower, and reading. Never anything different from the last twenty-five years of Steve's life. Not a thing, except the incredible urge to run, hide, or hang himself. The damnable misery of it all was the fact he brought others into his web of weakness. Angie, and now a child, were stuck in this life because he simply couldn't do the one thing Arthur had preached from the moment he joined: keep his dick in his pants.

In several ways, it seemed Arthur was right. Not in the *women are inferior, nothing to respect except their work, they are the temptation of the devil* ways he always preached, but that weakness, in and of itself, only led to punishment and detriment. Steve couldn't fight his weakness, and it would cost him.

First of all, his life was going to be significantly different. There was no way around it. Either fatherhood, leaving the community, or forced expulsion were in his future, if not two or more of those. There was the other option, but he didn't want to entertain that.

His decision to pursue something with a woman led Angie down this road, too. There was really no way it could be pinned on her. The females were taught to follow their brother's lead without questioning. How could they draw the line when it came to sex? It was drilled into them to not fight their superiors, and by law of the Green's Bay Community, penis equaled power.

The teachings of the women's faith alone were contradictory in nature. Listen to everything a man said, always, unless he wants sex, then say no and refuse. Now, as Angie and Steve had discussed on several occasions, they did have the right. No one should have sex against their will. Rape was always wrong. But, so was sexual relations in any form. There wasn't a single act therein that was bounded in faith.

Given everything Arthur taught about abstinence and will, Steve found it hard to disagree that he wasn't right. One time. One moment of weakness. There were many more times, overall, but it only took one. And now, several lives were going to be fucked up because of it. All because he wasn't strong enough in the faith he claimed to love above it all.

What came next in their lives was about to be decided. Steve and Angie were meeting in the small forest at the far west side of the grounds. There was a weather tower that blocked anyone from inside of the building from seeing the small stretch they had to run across the lawn. Once in the wood, they had about fifty yards of free space, under the cover of their lord's divine creations of green, leafy life.

Angie arrived at 11:15pm, just as they had planned. Steve showed up over an hour earlier, not able to focus on his book, or relax enough to get rest. He walked the halls for a bit before finally going to the woods and finding a nice stump to sit on and breathe in the fresh African night air.

As usual, Angie pulled her hair down from its ponytail when she reached the meeting place. It swished and swept over her shoulders, making the moonlight flicker on her smooth, freckled skin. Steve's mouth watered at the site of her entering the thicket.

She hugged and kissed him when they greeted. As Angie backed away, she exhaled and said, "Let's talk to Father Arthur tomorrow about leaving. I think it's the best bet."

Steve nodded. "You think he will just allow us to walk free? We won't have to pay any penance?"

"He won't be happy. I doubt our lord is happy with us, either. Hopefully, he can send us on a path to redemption, and we can start this next chapter in our lives on the right path."

"You've always had the right words for me." Steve hugged Angie and ran his fingers through her silky hair. His heartbeat slowed while he held her. So did his mind. She was an oasis of solitude. Nothing else mattered but her when they were together. "I hope he follows along with it."

"Pack your things and be gone tomorrow. This is not the kind of behavior I like from my brothers and servants, but I appreciate the honesty and willingness to not allow the evil of your actions to continue infecting our community." Arthur sat behind his desk. His elbows rested on the desktop, and his hands were pressed together, fingertips against fingertips.

When Steve first broke the news, he swore he saw a flash of rage pulse through Arthur's eyes. He convinced himself his own eyes played tricks on him. Arthur was stern, and sometimes a dick, but he was never out of control. He had people, like Conner, to take care of those things for him.

"If either of you would ever like to join again, seeing the error of your ways and willing to make amends with your lord, it will have to be discussed and judged upon by my most trusted and myself. I will not guarantee readmission into our community, but I can say that outside of us, you can find your own salvation. Separately, as you know you cannot be together and find it."

Steve bit his lip but nodded in agreement. He couldn't deny finding surprise in Arthur's acceptance. He thought they would be met with far more resistance than a simple lecture and slight talking down to. He wanted it to remain that way, so he went along with the flow.

"Yes, sir. I understand. Thank you for all your years of guidance and love, Father Arthur." Steve meant that. Even with all his fear of how things were going to go in the conversation, he really respected and loved the man. He wouldn't have given so much of his life and devotion to him otherwise. Love, true love and a perfect partner, made him broadened his scope.

"You're welcome. I wish it had resonated more, for your soul's sake, but I'm glad you will carry the lessons along with you in your future travels. Also remember, readmission and status with us aside, once a member of Green's Bay, always a member. One can never unlearn the teachings of our lord."

The meeting ended with a hug between the men. Arthur never acknowledged Angie's presence.

Steve and Angie sat on the silver and electric blue bus together. It felt odd to them both to be around people so openly. The years they spent in the community had trained their minds to think a certain way, and this bucked against every bit of it.

Giggles erupted between them just by looking at each other. It was fun, and as Angie pointed out upon boarding, it felt *dirty*. They were like kids sneaking off for their first weekend together.

There was a surprising bit of sadness for Steve. He hated that he hadn't been allowed to tell his friends bye. As per orders by Arthur, they left after the meeting without letting the others on to their departure. He really wanted to give Jones a proper ending to their brotherhood and wish him the best. It was not to be, though.

Deep down, Steve didn't think any complaint was worth it. He got out with his girl. The only punishment came in the form of listening to the old man bitch for about twenty minutes. Losing out on saying goodbye to someone he wasn't even sure would miss him was nothing.

Steve had to admit he was nervous. Several people started over in life, with varying degrees of success. Not many did it twice, and even fewer did it at his age. By then, most men were settled down, and even had grandchildren. In all honesty, Steve may have grandkids, but he wouldn't know them, or their parents, if they ran over him with their car.

Angie, who had no children or family after her dad died a week after she turned nineteen in Cleveland, was excited. There was no fear or regrets. The only thing she could even think of was she wished she had started a family earlier. The glow on her face and pure happiness in her soul was infectious. She was warm and loving and radiant.

"What's the first thing you want to do?" she said to Steve.

"Eat a damn hamburger with mayonnaise, bacon, and extra pickles," he said.

"Really? We had hamburgers at the community. Every Wednesday was burger night, remember?"

Steve scoffed. "They were cardboard patties with ketchup. Those nasty things couldn't even be considered food."

"I'm surprised you don't want to do something else, like walk around the market, or see some of the attractions, or something we weren't allowed to do."

"I do want to walk around the market." Steve nodded. "That's where the hamburger will be."

Even Angie laughed then. She loved how quick-witted he was. It always led to surprising good times, even when things should've been terrible. It was one of a multitude of things she loved about him.

"Why? What did you have in mind to do first?" Steve said.

"I don't know, to be honest. I don't know what's near here or what we can afford." She brushed her hair from her face. The bus slowed at a stop and added two more passengers. "You never told me if Arthur gave us enough to live on or just make it for a few days."

"I got a good bit back. We can live pretty well without a paycheck for a couple weeks. Longer, if we don't go crazy."

The couple spent the rest of the afternoon riding around town, looking at all the new things the world offered. People had little rectangular phones they looked at almost constantly. Even the commoners who sold fish and wheat at the markets had them. Angie remembered the huge phones that came in the leather pouches and plugged into the cigarette lighter hole in a car and were expensive as hell to use. Those had just come out when she joined Green's Bay. These little things were crazy, though, and must've been free for them, given the way people were using them.

For a little while, the pair munched on some candied nuts and hunted some fresh hamburger. They found that but had a shockingly hard time finding pickles. The last vendor they ventured up to had them, though.

They found a sweet little hotel in town. In the room was a king-sized bed, which looked like a trampoline to them after sleeping in those twin beds for so many years, and it felt like lying in one of heaven's clouds. The bathroom had a wonderful bathtub with all sorts of natural soaps and cleaning products. That made Angie happy and excited to use them. Around the bend from the wall, the TV was bolted to was a micro-kitchen. There was a tiny stove and refrigerator. This made Steve happy and excited to use it.

When they first got in the room, Steve tossed the food in the fridge and poured a glass of water. He sat on the edge of the bed beside Angie, who was flipping through the hundreds of channels of cable TV.

There were so many things to see. Laugh tracks played behind a chubby dude arguing with his out-of-his-league wife. A well-built guy with a furrowed brow had an inner struggle, trying not to attack a man he just arrested. A handsome, but slight, man talked about politics, and on a few channels, a guy pointed at a screen and talked about the weather. All of it was so stimulating to them both.

"You gonna go take a bath?" he said, rubbing his hand through her hair.

"I think so. I had thought about waiting until after dinner, but I'm having trouble getting it out of my mind."

"You should, then. It won't take long to cook dinner. I can bring it to you when it's ready, or I can come get you."

"Come get me. I'll eat with you."

She ran her bath water, and Steve sat on the bed. From where he sat in the middle of the bed, he could see her sexy, wet body in the tub. She lathered her body and smiled at Steve, teasing him and playing with his desires.

After a bit, Steve went into the kitchen and got everything going. He cooked the burgers to a beautiful medium and let them rest while he prepared the fixings and rounded up his love.

They ate in silence. Sometimes, Angie would ask a question, but Steve would only nod or shake his head. Both enjoyed dinner so much they didn't want to speak. Soon, they finished and talked for a short time.

Then, out of nowhere, Steve said, "Do you hear that?"

"Hear what, babe?" Angie looked up at him and made a straining face, as if squinting her eyes would help her.

"That noise. It sounds like scratching or rattling or something." He walked around the room, searching behind any closet doors and in the shower. The noise evaded his identification, so he turned to look at Angie and shrugged. "I guess I'm going crazy."

"There's no telling, to be honest. We're in a hotel. It could be rats, or squirrels, or little orphaned children. We may never know." Angie patted his hand.

They talked some more before lying down in bed. Steve, after a big, perfect meal, began dozing off in no time. Angie drifted in and out, being set at ease by her partner's deep, measured breathing.

A hand gripped Angie's hair, and jerked her, not only off Steve's chest, but also out of her dream world with violence she hadn't experienced since her father died. Her neck cracked, and something between her shoulders popped, sending sharp, searing pain down her spine.

She expected Steve to be the one holding her hair. Sometimes, he liked it rough, and liked to control, so she had no way to refuse him. The complete dominance of his actions was a turn on for them both.

But, it wasn't Steve. He lay on the ground beside her, bleeding, face down. Conner, who looked angrier than she'd ever seen a person, was holding her by the hair, like a magician pulls a trick bunny from a top hat. Angie jerked and flailed, kicking her legs and swinging her arms, hoping to make contact with anything on Conner that would cause him to let go.

"Stop it. Stop it, bitch!" he yelled. He shook his hand and blood, presumably Steve's, flung from his fingertips.

"What do you want?" screamed Angie. She still jerked around and wrestled him. "Arthur let us go! What the hell do you want with us?"

"I changed my mind," said Arthur, stepping from the bathroom. A loud electrical click came in the room with him. In his hand, Angie noticed a stun gun.

"You asshole!" she spat at him. Her eyes swam in tears of anger and pain.

Conner punched her in the side of the head. Her vision blurred, and she teetered on the edge of consciousnesses. It felt like her heartbeat started in her face. Her body went rigid, and a small cry leaked from her lips.

"I'm sorry, Father," said Conner.

"Don't be silly, my son. She deserved that. She can't keep getting by with bullshit. To be honest, too, I have grown tired of her thinking she can speak to me, or anyone of her brothers, in any way she pleases. I'll not be called names without repercussion."

"I feel the same," agreed Conner.

"You're such a kiss ass," mumbled Angie. The world around her was clearing up. She knew what was going on, and the danger she was in, but this time she simply didn't give a fuck. Arthur had lied to them. Conner had hit her. Trying to be diplomatic and leave the community on peaceful terms was out the window. She refused to keep her mouth shut any longer. "You better hope I don't get a hold of you under different circumstances, Conner. All of your bitch brothers may be scared of you, but I'm not."

He punched her three times, square in the middle of her forehead each time. Her head jolted back, and everything went blurry again before winking out entirely.

"Get them to the van," said Arthur. "We need to get out before the sire of the whore's offspring comes to."

All hell broke loose when Conner tried dragging Steve through the bay doors leading to the basement. Everything had gone so well. The couple didn't move an inch the entire trip from the hotel to Green's Bay. The moment Conner opened the back doors of the van, though, Steve jumped out on him like a rabid cat.

Conner screamed, obviously scared by the surprise. Arthur, on the other hand, didn't even flinch. He gripped the handle on the flapping passenger door of the van and slammed it into the side of Steve's head.

Steve reeled and slumped over. It took a moment for Conner to regain his bearings, but when he did, he climbed on top of Steve and pummeled him. His face looked like raw beef with a thick trail of blood running from it. He still had eyes, but they were swollen shut. His nose was there, but it was little more than a bump on a puffy and bruised mound of flesh.

"That's enough, Conner. Get him in," instructed Arthur.

Arthur grabbed a handful of Angie's hair and pulled her from the floor of the van. Her bones clunked, and her skin smacked on the concrete. He loved feeling the friction of the rough, pebbly ground tearing her flesh.

Conner threw Steve on a gurney and tied his arms and legs down. Steve had no clue as the straps rubbed burns on to his skin. Some sick pleasure within Conner made him tighten the restraints until he physically couldn't do so anymore. The sadist in him was fully awakened in the moment.

Angie's hair pulled out from the roots. It was a turn of events that served to piss Arthur off. Her hair broke free from her scalp, and it caused him to drop her. He cussed and kicked her in the shoulder twice out of anger.

"Dumb ... whore!" he shouted with each thrust of his stubby leg. "Conner, pick this bitch up and take her to room 23-A."

Conner nodded and pulled Angie's limp body on to his shoulders in a fireman's carry. Her head, hair, and limbs flopped around like they were made of rubber.

While he carried her down the hall, Arthur examined Steve. He was beaten rather severely. He would require a substantial amount of healing time before being integrated back into the community, if he was found worthy enough. His face looked like Bell's Palsy affected it. The left side around the mouth and the cheek beneath his eye was taut and frozen.

Conner stomped into the loading area, huffing and with his brow furrowed. His discontent influenced his body language. The jerky way he moved and the aggressiveness in his gait gave away how much he wanted to harm someone.

Arthur noticed the man's growing tension. "My boy," he started, "have a drink of water and unwind a bit. I need you to be clear-headed."

"I'm okay, Father."

Arthur couldn't suppress his laugh. He shook his head and said, "Son, you're a powder keg, filled with gasoline, and smoking a cigar. I understand why. You've made your loyalty to me well-known, but you need a moment to decompress. These two have gotten deep under your skin."

"They have. Their fucking blatant, flippant disrespect is overwhelming to me. And to top it all off, they had the pure audacity to fight back. We should've found them hanging in the closet from committing suicide in shame. Instead, we find them in after-coitus bliss and sinful sleep. They're wastes of time and love."

"I know, son, which is why I need you to be on your game. You get too wrapped up in your own head sometimes, and violence clouds your mind. Violence, while not as bad as the sin that finds these two in their places, is a sin, too. Don't allow it to taint your soul."

Conner didn't argue. He knew that Arthur was right, after all. His temper had always been his downfall. Even before joining the community, the church he attended spoke to his parents about praying his anger away. When he almost beat the pastor's daughter to death in a co-ed baseball game for not running out the bases, they banished his family from the church. His dad was ashamed of him and set out to make Conner's life hell afterwards. He beat the boy every day for some dumb ass reason or another until the day Conner found his temper again, and let it go on his father.

His dad walked into the kitchen where Conner was making his typical breakfast of toast with butter and grape jam. Every morning, his dad ate the same thing and had Conner make it for him. It was a bit demeaning to be nineteen years old and forced to make his father's breakfast before he left for work, but it wasn't something he made common knowledge, either.

When Conner slid the paper towel with the four slices of toast across the table, his dad grabbed his wrist. He had enough pressure in his grip Conner could feel the multiple bones and joints in his wrists crunching together. Conner tried to pull his arm away from his father, but he was having none of it.

"What's wrong, Pop?" The tentativeness in his body leaked out in his voice. His shifty eyes also betrayed him.

"What do you think is wrong?"

"I don't know, or I wouldn't have asked."

The flash in his father's eyes told Conner he had fucked up. "Look, you little asshole, you know you burnt this toast."

"It got a little darker than usual. Something went wrong. I put extra butter on it to make it better."

"You can eat it. Make me some more. The right way."

"We don't have any more bread."

His dad evaluated the information for a moment. "Scrape the black off and put new topping on it."

Conner breathed in a steadying breath. He wanted to keep his cool, but his dad was pushing his power.

"What's wrong? Don't like being talked down to? Well, guess what? After your little stunt with Pastor Fairweather's daughter, that's all this town does to me. They talk down to me for raising such a little, angry, violent son of a bitch."

"I ... couldn't ... help ... it." grunted Conner. His teeth were clenched, and the muscles in his arms twitched.

"Poor thing. Couldn't help having a temper tantrum and beating some girl an inch from her life because she didn't take a ballgame as serious as you did. I guess you're the victim in all this? God, I hate you."

That was all it took. Conner had heard that last line enough from everyone around him. The Fairweather girl said it, too, right before he exploded. His father told him at least three times a day. He wasn't going to hear it anymore.

Conner unplugged the toaster from the wall. He wrapped the cord around his hand five times and palmed the hot base with a wet dish rag. Steam floated from the hot metal.

His father looked at him as he swung the appliance at his face. The thud of the metal pounding into the old man's face, and the sizzle of the toaster on his skin, might have made anyone around sick to their stomach.

Not Conner. He was incensed. He wanted to beat the man to death. He was no longer his father. He was no more than an obstacle between him and happiness, and Conner wasn't going to be unhappy anymore.

The toaster bent and came apart in pieces. Soon, Conner was swinging nothing more than the still-hot coils of the inside. Blood and flesh from his father's face flew from each blow Conner gave, until the old guy slumped over and fell to the floor from the rickety wooden chair he took his brutalization in.

Heaving over his father's gurgling body, Conner began to giggle. He felt happier than he had in years, really since his last outburst with the preacher's daughter. Free. Alive. Blood pumped through his veins. Pores opened up to allow sweat and air to pass through. The fine hairs on his neck stiffened and were stalks growing from his skin. His brain processed every sound and smell and feeling like it never had before. He knew everything in the moment. He lived. For the first time in his life, he really lived.

That feeling was a drug. It was as addictive as any pill, or alcohol, or substance anyone ever put into their body. He had tried them all, and none of them had the impact beating his father's skull in hand. Sex never gave him the release that did. Not even fucking close. He needed violence.

When he learned of Arthur's community, and that he could find salvation through his teachings and abstinence, he knew he had found his home. The flier that went out to the anger program the court ordered for him was asking for guards. Not guards in the traditional sense, but general population, undercover guards. It fit Conner's needs perfectly.

To Africa he went, in two days' time. One phone call with the old man and he said to hell with everything. His house, his probation, everything. He didn't plan on coming back, so it had no bearing on the rest of his life. From that day on, he was Arthur's number-one disciple.

Arthur knew what he was doing. He was never afraid of the boy's temper, nor his past. He needed that. He even searched for that, along with a young, impressionable mind that he could mold and make into whatever he wanted. Conner would become an important part of what Arthur was building.

He did. Conner grew into the best person Arthur ever recruited. He didn't know just how well he would work out. Now, the boy trusted Arthur without question. He got upset anytime someone bucked against Arthur's word, like it was a slap in his own face. He was a great soldier, and one Arthur grew to be quite fond of. That was something Arthur didn't say about many people.

Although he told Conner to go calm down, he didn't want him to lose his fire. He needed the boy to be clear-headed enough to be at his violent best. Arthur had seen him in this shape in the past and knew he would do him no good. All he wanted was to cause pain, and he knew from experience Conner wouldn't give a damn if he killed, not until after, anyway.

Arthur wanted these two alive, though. They would be important in the next phase of lessons for the colony. Conner could beat them all he wanted. Recovery time meant nothing to the old man. What mattered was obedience and subservience. He would restore that over his community by any means necessary.

Steve heard screaming. Everything felt so foggy, he was unsure if he dreamed it or if it were real.

The inside of his head felt like he was underwater. Everything was muffled and deadened in his ears. His eyes were struggling to focus on anything, but the edges of the walls and ceilings were sharpening as time slugged by.

The screaming, though, that got louder. The more his head woke up, and things became clearer and made more sense, words began to register.

"Hell! Hell! See! He was me!"

What the hell does that mean, Steve wondered. More than that, who was it, and why couldn't they shut the hell up until after his head quit throbbing?

"Hell! Um Hell. Nick!"

Who the hell was Nick, and who was fucking screaming?

Steve tried to sit up and realized then, he was strapped down to a hospital bed. A cheap, musty, rickety one from some time in the early 1900's. It cracked and popped every time he jerked at his restraints. Stranger than that, he was naked, and his inner thighs and balls hurt.

Strength was in poor supply, but Steve thought he could possibly break the ties holding him down, or at least the bed that they were attached to. Even with his weakness, he felt the frame of the bed was weaker.

After some steadying breaths, and blocking out the nerve-wracking screams, he began to tug at each one of the ties to feel for the one he had the best chance to break free from. When he pulled at the one holding down his left leg, the bed popped, and his leg flew up into the air. Hanging on the end of the faded, yellow strap was a rusted and jagged piece of metal. It used to be a piece of the frame, and if Steve could get it in his hand, it would be a tool.

He wriggled and got his free foot wedged in the handles on the side of the bed. Bracing and using it for leverage, he pulled with all his might at the restraint. He held his breath and grunted with exertion, and finally, with a much louder snap than before, his hand came loose.

Stars swam in his eyes, and a fresh sting of pain shot across the top of his head when he breathed again. Dizziness took hold of him for a moment, and he took time to regain his bearings.

The screaming came back. It made sense, now, too.

"Help! Help, Steve. He's hurting me! Come, quick!"

It was Angie, and he was stronger in an instant. Adrenaline raced through his body, and he thought he could kill everyone and everything that was between her and he.

The other hand came loose from the bed with all-but no power. It had all the resistance swinging his arm under water. His remaining tied-up leg didn't even register in his raging body. He just got the hell up, ripping the leg free, and went to take care of business.

Nothing mattered to him. Not where he was. Not that he was naked. Not that the pain in his groin was so intense he could barely stand. Nothing, except getting to Angie.

"Stop! Stop it, asshole!"

Steve almost lost the contents of his stomach. A silent tear came from his eye when he broke through the door and into the long, dusty hall. He noted its blue, tile floor, and wide, metal doors on either side before the world crashed into the side of his head.

Everything swirled in his eyes and blurred into undefinable blobs. The floor rose up and smacked him square in his face. His nose bled, and stinging stars took over his vision. Breathing was almost impossible. The breath leaving his body rippled the small amount of blood pooling around his mouth. Footsteps echoed in the hall and popped in his ears.

Conner looked down at Steve as he passed out. The son of a bitch would have to learn the hard way.

When Angie came to, excruciating pain mauled her lower abdomen. Between her hips felt like someone let a wolverine loose inside her. She couldn't even lift herself up. Her thighs ached every time her brain sent a signal to her muscles. Just the thought of them moving made them sear and radiate pain. Her bones felt like they separated from her muscle, or they were tearing away each time she tried moving.

Heaviness settled on everything in the room, including her subconscious. The stainless steel, rolling surgical table, the IV rod attached to the ugly, tan, exam bed, and the blue box with the silver face, all had a deep sadness and trauma resting upon them, like humidity in the summer.

The room's white walls were bathed in dinginess, grime, and age. The Green's Bay Community building had its own feel of history and wealth of background, but this was different. This room looked to be built with the same 1920's style the community building had been updated from. A blanket of nightmares lay upon the room, though. Many lifetimes of them, in fact.

Angie shook off a shudder at the thought of the lives ruined in the room she occupied. Even in the back of her mind, she wondered was her's one of them. The pain coursing through her made her want to travel down that rabbit hole. She could also remember what her father said about her cousin, Sheila, not recalling his multiple sexual assaults on her: sometimes, not remembering can be a blessing.

The heavy metal door creaked open. Arthur came in, reading the second page of a stack stapled together at the top left corner. Angie, to her own surprise, was comforted by his presence. It may have been just the sight of someone familiar, or lingering faith in him and his love over the last decade of her life, something of a nostalgic feeling in the appearance of the man she followed for so long without question.

All of that flushed from her when Conner came through the door behind Arthur. All the memories, the fears, the pain, the betrayal, replaced the safety foolishly budding inside her.

Angie recoiled away from them. The quick violence of the action made pain sear within her body. Because of that, she winced and curled into a fetal position.

"Oh, are you in pain?" said Arthur.

Angie nodded as tears dripped from her nose onto the rubber mattress.

"Good. Pain is the physical form of remorse. Maybe you will learn something from it."

Arthur refused to look away from his papers as he spoke.

Conner, on the other hand, drilled into her with his gaze. She could feel him inside her, even with her eyes closed and trying to forget where she was. "Fucking slut," he said.

"Although your language leaves something to be desired, my son, there can be nothing to look down on in your truth. Though, I believe it could be put in a more intellectual way, even she can't argue your point," said Arthur.

Silence settled over the room for a moment. Tiniest of whimpers slipped from Angie's chapped lips. Breaths that delivered a faint growl came from Conner's chest. Nothing abnormal happened with Arthur. He was his usual, nonchalant self. The amount of pain Angie was in had no bearing on him in any way.

Conner broke the silence soon. "Do you argue that?"

It didn't dawn on Angie that his question was meant for her, until he punched her in the stomach. She thought he could've reached up inside of her and jerked her intestines out and it hurt less. The pain went so deep, her soul was in critical condition. Her head hung over the edge of the bed, and vomit spewed from her mouth.

Shocking even Conner, Arthur pushed him

away from her. "Leave her be," he scolded. "That's going to kill her. She's still recovering."

"Yes, sir. I'm sorry."

Arthur shook his head. "No, son. No need to apologize. You need to keep your temper in check. Just because her disrespect of you deserved it, doesn't mean you need to let it get to you that much."

"It pisses me off so much."

"I get it, but I can't keep having this talk with you. You need to learn when and when not to use this temper of yours."

Conner nodded, and his lip stuck out, like a kid.

"You should answer the man's question," Arthur directed at Angie. "Just because you're weak doesn't give you a legitimate reason to disregard a question from your superior."

Angie held her stomach. The pain was more than anything she ever felt. It seemed to seep into her very spirit and wreak havoc on her psyche. All of her resolve and strength poured from her body like sand from an hourglass. Soon, the cavern left behind took over. It spoke around her pain, even around her own mind. It took control of her, in an act of self-preservation.

"No, sir. It's true. I am a ... fucking slut," she whimpered.

"Now, now," said Arthur, "you are right."

Conner wondered why the sudden change in Arthur's demeanor toward her. He was sweet and caring. He even petted her shoulder when he spoke to her. Conner never saw Arthur even address a woman unless he needed service.

Arthur turned away from Angie and went out the door without another word. Conner sped along after him after he realized he was leaving the room. They only made it a few steps from Angie's door before Conner's curiosity got the better of him.

"Father, I'm sorry to question you, but why are you so nice to her now, after what she's done to you and our community?"

"Because now, she's broken. I believe we have nothing to worry about from her now. She will be a good servant of the Green's Bay Community from now on."

Conner opened the door to the stairwell and allowed Arthur to pass through, thinking how much sense his leader's words made.

Not quite six weeks later, everyone gathered in the dinner hall. The guys laughed and talked about their day and took the piss out of each other with inside jokes within their little fraternities. Jovial moments passed between the boys over canned veggies and the kitchen staff's choice of protein, like every other day.

The women sat in their usual place behind the food station. They spoke and shared soft smiles. All of them possessed a mousy nature.

Steve sat in front of his tray. The things he'd gone through to this point taught him how to act. Shut the hell up, smile when needed, nod when prompted, and keep his dick in his pants.

The latter of those was easy to do now. Even if he took it out and whipped it around in front of everyone, he couldn't do anything with it. It was little more than a dangling flap of skin. After talking to Arthur, he learned what his penance for sinning was. His penis and balls had basically been electrocuted until they were dead. His cock had no feeling in it. He stroked it and smacked it and pinched it, and nothing. Not a thing. His balls quit producing testosterone. There was no desire for sex. His fire and will to be a respected male were depleted. Even the hair on his arms and legs was falling out.

Angie didn't even speak to the other women. They didn't know the level of evil leading them. Terror built in her every day she woke up, and she realized she hadn't been having a huge, horrible nightmare. Her days were spent locked up in debilitating fear. Any time Arthur or Conner were around her; her insides became one giant knot. She did the things she had to do to stay alive and out of pain, to the point she hadn't so much as looked at Steve since their last day in the hotel.

Arthur told the community that they were sick and quarantined. Everyone was welcoming and happy to see them when they were integrated back into the general population. Smiles and handshakes met Steve upon his return. Nods and simple gestures of acknowledgment greeted Angie, which suited her fine.

There wasn't enough understanding among the community for Arthur, though. Steve and his whore understood it fine. He could tell that by the way they reacted to him. He wondered, because of the story related to the community, did everyone else get the importance of no sex.

Arthur had a plan, and that dinner was the perfect time to implement it. Excitement rushed through his body as the time drew near. The presentation was going to be strong and have a lasting impact. He loved things like that. He loved being at the center of their creation. It's what made him worthy of his role.

As everyone sat back in their chairs, or rubbed their stomachs, or moaned in bliss from fullness after a long day, Arthur took the moment. It was the right time, before folks began filing out of the dinner hall.

"Hey, children," Arthur shouted after clapping his hands. "I have something to say, so if you could, please, take a minute to learn with me."

All of the people sat up and feigned alertness while trying to come out of their food comas. Some looked interested to see what came. Arthur noted these as the members of the community with the least amount of guilt.

"We've had a good response with you all learning and repenting for your various sins. Some have put their heads down and really turned themselves around. For you, I am truly grateful. You all are the ones sent by God. You make me love being his mouth, his eyes, and his finger.

"There are others, though, whom I'm afraid still haven't learned the errors of their actions. You are the ones that lead to long nights of me begging for the right answers from our lord. You are the ones who make me question myself. You are the reason I feel like a failure.

"You are the reason we're here."

Arthur went into the janitor's closet located behind his table. He opened the door and pulled out blue box on wheels with a towel over some kind of container sitting on the top. The box began humming after he plugged it in. All the eyes in the dinner hall were wide and glued on the old man.

"Things need to be clear that the greatest sin or the abominations that are rendered from the actions will not be tolerated here. There is no reason or excuse for this slip up. It will not go unpunished anymore."

Arthur slid the towel from the humming, blue box, revealing a thick jar with dark, cloudy liquid in it. He put both hands around it and placed it on his table. Everyone was so intent and on edge. The atmosphere dripped with tension. Arthur loved every moment of it.

"This is where our lesson will begin, and the message should sink in," Arthur said. He grabbed a long set of tongs from the food station and took the lid off the jar.

Arthur eased the tongs down into the disgusting juice and fished around to get a good hold on something swirling around in the bottom. He angled his arm upward and clamped down on whatever he was after and used his other hand to secure his grip. When he extracted the target from the jar, the whole room lost its air. Stifled. Strangled.

What lay on a dinner tray on the old man's table was a red and tanned bundle of flesh. Some of the skin had begun to blacken. The liquid it came from made the wrinkled mass glisten in the fluorescent lights of the dinner hall. Trails of moisture ran along the folds and onto the towel Arthur placed the thing on.

He took some of the excess towel and patted the blob of skin, drying it, and cleaning it a little. There was a resemblance to a whole chicken. Its arms and legs bent and drew up to its body, but its bulbous head rolled around on a neck that only attached to the body by skin. The face hadn't defined to any sort of noticeable features.

That didn't deter the realization of Angie. It was her unborn baby. The one Arthur stole from her abdomen by force. The one she still felt inside her, if nothing but a remembrance in pain. The child she loved.

"This is the physical form of sin," Arthur said. He turned the knobs on the blue box and the humming radiated in louder waves. "This is the abominations in which bring man down and make them unable to reach their highest potential. The opportunity is there, given by God. As men, we must abstain and refrain. This is our downfall.

"To show you all how devoted I am to your

salvation, I will take it upon myself to chase the evil out. It will take so much out of me, but the purity for this community and the souls of the people in it means I must take this burden on."

Arthur pulled the nodes from the side of the blue box and secured them on either side of the fetus. He pressed a button and electrical current flowed through the lifeless body. Cracking and popping came from the table, and the tiny mass of human shook violently.

People in the dinner hall watched. Some glazed over at the sight, no longer comprehending. They checked out. The trauma being too much for them.

Others sweated, or cried, or gritted their teeth. The scene before them attacked their nerves and stability.

Everyone watching was on the verge of breaking. No one was prepared for something like that. No one could prepare for something like that. The fetus was smoking from the amount of electricity being forced through it. Even though they all knew it felt nothing, everyone in the room felt its pain and horror.

Arthur wanted to laugh out loud. His presentation was making its mark on everyone. Not an eye in the room retained a single shred of sanity. He was taking over their minds. His loss of humanity gained unbridled control.

Now was not the time to crack in his victory. The game must be played through to have the lasting impact he wanted. Laughing would ruin the facade he'd built over how hard the torture took out of him. He enjoyed it so much that the only thing that made him stop was when the towel caught fire beneath the body.

Conner came in and doused the flaming fabric with the cooler of powdered lemonade they had all drank with dinner. The fetus fell to the floor in the wave of drink. A thud and smack in the midst of the splash broke the nail-biting, incredible silence in the room.

The fetus lay on the floor, and the air stank with the odor of burnt baby, fear, and disbelief. The veins that were just growing through the body when it was snatched from its mother sparked with electrical current. Each time it did, the body would coil into a tighter ball, and release the tension when the aftershocks passed through.

"Tell me, now, do you all understand the magnitude of the unforgivable sin?" said Arthur. A maniacal look in his eyes were the only thing betraying his stoic face.

The words he spoke had a jarring effect on most. The majority of the members watching had mentally vacated the room. They were there, but they weren't living in the moment.

The brutal and sickening display before them had made their brains run as far away from that dinner hall as they could get. But, they came back when Arthur spoke, and almost out of instinct, they nodded in acknowledgment. Everyone gave some sort of recognition and gesture of agreement. All of them had learned a hard lesson and would follow Arthur no matter the level of depravity, for the fear settled in deep.

Everyone, but Angie.

III

The men were instructed to go to their rooms, and the women were made to clean up the sticky, fake lemonade on the floor. They mopped and scrubbed the sugary mess and cleaned the food station in preparation for breakfast the following day. Conner and Arthur wheeled the blue box away down the hall after Conner grabbed the fetus with the tongs and tossed it into a plastic trash bag and took it with them.

Angie went to the adjacent kitchen and wrote a note: MEET ON ROOF @ 2AM

When she came out of the kitchen, Steve was in the line waiting to get out of the metal double doors. All the fellows in the group were still shaken, and in no real hurry to spend time alone with the memories of the dead baby being shocked until it burst into flames.

At first, the old ideal of trying to be slick took hold. It was the first time Angie looked at Steve in months. It would draw attention if she walked up to him. She realized at that very moment she no longer gave two flying fairies fucking on a farm what anyone liked.

Arthur's demonstration changed everyone. It left a scar on each person in the dinner hall. For Angie, the change went the opposite way Arthur intended. She had been beaten into complete and total submission. She hadn't even spoken in six weeks and would've been okay if she was never required to speak again as long as she lived. But in her case, it made her come alive.

The woman's resilience rushed in like a riptide on the front end of a CAT 5 hurricane. Her need for revenge outweighed the need to breathe. Angie was a different person.

In front of everyone in the room, she walked up to Steve, tapped him on the arm, and handed him the note she had written.

A couple of people noticed the interaction, but everyone was really too shell-shocked and traumatized to care much. With Arthur and Conner gone already, there wasn't anybody to be afraid of seeing.

Steve's face shuffled through a thousand emotions upon laying eyes on her. At first confusion, then fear, anger, and he came to rest on the saddest, most heartbreaking look she'd ever seen on him. Angie knew then he recognized their baby, too. The urge to hold him and cry together, hard, hit her like a ten-ton brick.

As Steve opened his mouth to speak, Angie turned away and went to the kitchen. She went straight to the pantry where they kept all the huge cans of vegetables. There was no way in hell she would help clean up the mess. Those two sons of bitches could come to the pantry and beat and shoot her. It didn't mean shit. If she saw either of them at that moment, they wouldn't make it out of the pantry in one piece.

The fire she hadn't felt since her teens raged inside of her. The emptiness left by her baby was replaced with the desire for reckoning. She wanted pain. She wanted blood. She wanted Arthur's life.

Steve debated with himself over whether or not he should meet with Angie. They both knew it was dangerous. There would never be a good time for the two to meet again, but after what they just saw, now was a really damn bad time. Plus, it was the first time she even looked at him, and the shock was reeling.

Whatever it was, Steve knew it had to be important. Most likely, it was something about their unborn baby being the subject of heinous torture. The devilish show had scarred everyone in the community. It must've fucked the mother up more than anyone.

As the mind often does, Steve's tried to venture off to less terrible causes for Angie's request to meet. Maybe since Arthur and Conner were gone, she felt like she had a safe opening to address him. It could've been that she wanted to talk to him and tell him that wasn't their child, not to worry. His masculine-driven thoughts even wondered was it because six weeks had passed, and she wanted sex she didn't know he couldn't perform.

The last idea was foolish, but he wanted anything to be the case rather than forcing himself to process what he just saw. He watched that fetus shake and burn. That fetus was his baby, no matter how much he wanted to believe it wasn't. He watched the man whom he loved and admired for over twenty years, torture the corpse of the child he took from him.

This made Steve's knees weak. His legs barely moved him forward. They resisted every motion his brain forced through them. Tendons burned fighting his movements. Ligaments stretched and pulled. The only emotion he felt was fear locking his body up inside.

Against everything within him telling him not to, he decided to meet her that night. After he learned what she needed, if he wasn't killed by Arthur or Conner for being caught, then he may make a break for it and run until he was caught, or no one could ever find him.

Clouds covered most of the moonlight and all of the stars. Toward the east, the golden bubble of the city lights made a dome on the horizon. A warm breeze blew in from the west off the ocean miles away. Tears spilled onto Angie's cheeks, and the gentle wind dried them within seconds.

Anticipation gnawed at Angie's stomach. She wondered if Steve would come. If he did come, she worried they would be caught. That would ruin everything. All she could do was wait. Every minute that passed felt like five lifetimes.

The door of the stairwell opened at 2:07. The scrape and squeak that used to signal a good time was now a signal for uncertainty and anxiety. All Angie could do was wait to see who walked around the corner.

It was Steve, but he didn't have his familiar happiness and calm. His face showed how terrified he was with every step, and how hyper-aware he was of everything going on. The edge of panic loomed ever so close, and his body language snitched him out.

Before she could say a word, Steve blurted out, "What in the hell is going on? You're gonna get us killed. Have you not seen how crazy they are?" He looked over his shoulder twice as he spoke.

As much as Angie loved that man, the fiery

flames of hell flew through her. "Hell yes, I've seen and felt how goddamn crazy they are. Did you not see what happened tonight? That was my baby ... our baby, that old motherfucker ripped from my body." Her voice cracked, and tears began falling in earnest.

Steve reached to put his arms around her, but she smacked him in the chest and face.

"No!" she yelled. "No! Get your damn hands off me. No other man will put his hands on me without my permission, including you!"

Steve put both his hands up where she could see them both and backed away. He was already a nervous wreck when he showed up. Angie was making things ten times worse.

"Yes, yes. I understand, Angie. I'm sorry." Steve worked to make his voice calm. It was more of a fight than he expected.

She continued swinging and flailing at him until she wore herself down and collapsed, heaving and in tears.

Steve caught her. After what she just said, it scared him to do so, but instinct took over. He couldn't let her fall on her face. Also, it was damn near impossible not to console her.

"I'm sorry, Ang. I'm sorry." He rubbed her head while her body shook from her breathless sobs.

Inside, Angie's chest burned, and a painful stitch poked into her right side. It felt like she may never get her breath back.

Minutes, that took as long as hours, went by. Steve knew he needed to be with her, to see her through the other side, but the anxiety that went away with her breakdown was building back in.

"Hey, babe, I think we need to move or—"

"No. I'm not running anymore. I'm not avoiding them anymore. It all changes. Right now."

"What do you mean?" Angie pulled away, so Steve let go of her.

"I mean I'm leaving this place. I'm either walking out, or I'm being sent out in a bag, but I'll not be living here this time tomorrow." Her jaw set in a hard line, and her eyes were cold and hard as steel. "And if you want to stand in my way, you'll be the first one I go through."

Steve stood back and appraised the woman he loved. As long as he'd known her, she never spoke or acted like that. She took him aback, and he was unsure how to approach the situation.

"You can stare all you want. All I need is an answer."

The tone of her voice was violent in and of itself. This woman, although the same one Steve loved, was changed. Her strength flared from her in waves of heat on her skin. Fearlessness radiated from her, but more than that, she felt dangerous. Her energy was reminiscent of a bomb counting down, and Steve had all ideas when she detonated she was changing as many lives as she could.

"Ang, I have no intentions of standing in your way, no matter what you do. I just want to make sure you're safe."

"There isn't a thing safe in this equation. The only way to be safe is to get the fuck away from here."

"I know that. I've seen how insane Arthur is firsthand. Are you sure this is the right course to take, though?"

"No. Hell no. I'm not sure of a damn thing, except I don't live here anymore."

"That's what I mean, Ang. You might not be living at all."

"I'm well aware of that, and I'm prepared for it. They already took my child, they took you. If they take my life, it won't hurt half as bad as what I watched at dinner."

Steve nodded. Although some part of him wanted to live in denial about it being their child, he knew better. He couldn't watch it, and he didn't even carry the baby. He knew it must've torn Angie into emotional shreds.

"I won't stand in your way," Steve said. "I'll stand beside you, just like I always have."

Angie looked at him. Maybe she would have smiled from her appreciation of him, but there wasn't shit worth smiling over. Two months ago, Angie was a girlfriend and expecting mother. Now, she was preparing to kill.

"So, what's the first step?" Steve said. He followed her through the door into the stairwell. He knew it was her show, and he was allowed to be part of it.

It was a struggle to keep up with her. Her walk was more of a march. She thundered forward, like a linebacker blitzing a quarterback. Her mission overtook her body's demeanor.

"I'm hoping we'll run into Conner first. I think he's our biggest physical threat."

"Do I need to remind you the wrong Arthur put us through?" Steve felt his broken dick twinge when he referred to the impotence-inducing torture he went through after being brought back to the community.

"No," she said, "but you need to remember to keep your mouth shut sometimes. Your foot flies right in there when you open it so much."

Angie's newfound aggression was both attractive and off-putting. He liked it, but he wasn't accustomed to it. Her taking charge attitude was sexy, though. There was a bit of it that reminded him of his first wife and mother. Strong women had always turned him on. The problem with Angie was there was a slight, chaotic danger bubbling beneath the surface.

The two of them made their way down the stairs. It alarmed Steve that Angie didn't slow at all as they passed the fourth floor, then the third, then the second. She made a beeline for the first floor, where most of the members of the community and Arthur's rooms were located.

"Are you sure the direct approach is best?" Steve's nerves got the best of him.

"Stop asking dumbass questions."

Steve noted her voice's harsh snap. It crawled down his spine, sprouting goosebumps on his skin, like tiny mole hills. For the first time, he had to admit, Angie intimidated him.

Angie opened the door to the landing of the first floor and stomped out. The door swung back and slapped Steve in the arm. Angie was almost at the kitchen before Steve came out of the stairwell.

"Come on," Angie directed. She stopped and waited for him to catch up to her before she entered the kitchen.

When they went in, Angie went straight for the cutlery box. She pulled two huge knives and a heavy, steel meat cleaver. She handed the knives to Steve, who took them with all the hesitance one would a baby wrapped in a bomb and trotted off a huge cabinet on the wall.

"What do you want me to do with these?"

"If you don't know an answer to that," Angie

started, "just hold on to them for me."

When she opened the door of the cabinet, a light blue soufflé torch rolled out and hit her in the chest. Although it startled her, she caught it before it hit the ground, which relieved Steve. He didn't want the clatter to echo down the hall and alert anyone.

Angie tucked the torch into the waistband of her pants, like an old west cowboy carrying a gun. She reached back in the cabinet and pulled out a thick, cast iron frying pan. It was a smaller one, maybe six inches in diameter, the kind Steve's grandmother used to cook cornbread in. She smiled and shut the cabinet door.

"What now?" Apprehension carried Steve's voice.

"Follow me," she said, as she slid out of the kitchen into the hallway again.

They followed the corridor past a couple conference halls and offshoots to other wings of the building. On the corner of one of the openings was an ancient nurses' desk. It had a rusted chain link barrier from the desktop to the ceiling, with a steel-framed rectangle cut out along the front. Johnny, whose brother named Double A had got him into the community, slept in an office chair. Every time he sucked a deep snore, the chair squeaked beneath him.

"Shh," Steve warned, with his finger over his lips. "Don't wake him up."

"No shit," Angie smarted. "I thought about giving him a lap dance."

Steve shrugged and crouched down to follow Angie again, who traversed the hall like a soldier in stealth combat. Steve gripped the knives so tight that the feeling in his hands was being replaced with pin pricks. Sweat beaded on his scalp, and he had to make a conscience effort to breathe. It was no longer an involuntary action.

When they made it safely past Johnny, a bedroom door opened right before them. Joseph, Henry's former workmate, stepped out from the door.

"What are you two up to walking the halls at this time of night?" he said.

"I'm getting out of here. Steve is coming with me. You're welcome to join if you want," she said. "It's fair to tell you that Arthur has some things to answer for first."

"You're doing what?" Joseph rubbed his eyes with his knuckles, like it would speed the waking process.

"You heard me. Are you going to stand in our way?"

"I don't know what's gotten into you, but you don't speak to one of your superiors like this!" He shook his head and sighed.

Before Joseph had time to finish exhaling, Angie had snatched one of the knives from Steve and plunged it into his neck. When she jerked the blade from his skin, a fountain of blood shot up, and he collapsed to the floor.

"What the fuck is going on?" yelled Johnny, as he rounded the desk and approached them.

"I'm leaving," Angie said. It was calm, far too calm to be standing in an ever-growing pool of blood from a man she just killed. Chills ran along Steve's skin.

"You just killed brother Joseph! You're not going anywhere except Hell!" Johnny shouted, approaching Angie.

"I've been there," she said, and jammed the bloody knife in his left eye.

Screams from both him and Steve filled the corridor. They rushed down to the ends of the hall and bounced back to them, like ocean waves.

Angie twisted the knife in Johnny's eye, and he began convulsing and fell to the floor. On his way down, she ripped the knife from his face.

Steve's face was covered in terror. Angie grabbed him by the arm and pulled him into a janitor's closet beside the long-ago-abandoned nurse's desk. She shut the door and snapped the lock in place just as people were looking into the source of all the noise.

"Oh fuck. Oh fuck. Oh fuck!" Steve said. His voice shook and broke in his throat.

"Steve, I love you, and I want to be with you," she said, cupping his cheek in her hand and making him peer into her eyes. "But I need you get control of yourself, or you're going to be killed. Be the man I know. I need the strength. I need the father of my child. I need you to be the man that taught me how to stand up for myself."

"I didn't teach you how to murder!"

"There is no other way, and you know it," she said. She was gentle with him. "Think back to what you saw at dinner. You think there's another way to do this with people like that? Even if there was, I don't want my baby to go through that for nothing."

"I ...." Steve trailed off.

"Stop shutting it out. Allow yourself to see it. Really see it."

He closes his eyes, something he'd not done since dinner. The torture scene played over in his mind. Smoke and sparks arose from the tiny corpse. He watched but didn't see. Now, he felt it.

Steve started crying. His head dropped. Stuttered breaths fought to enter his chest. Sobs leaked from his tight lips.

"I know, baby. I know. Now, you know why I can't stay here."

"I want to go."

"Let's go, then," she said.

Angie opened the door just enough to peek out. There were only two men, Ted and Jeffery, standing in the hall. Down the wing opening, she could hear some others telling people to go to the dinner hall while they worked to clean the mess and find the killer.

"You ready now?" she asked Steve.

He nodded.

She swung the door open. Jeffery had his back to her, but Ted looked on from down the hall. Angie jumped out from the janitor's closet and sliced Jeffery's neck.

Ted charged at her, yelling from the trauma of what he witnessed. He launched himself at her when he was within five feet of her.

Angie froze, scared of how hard he would hit her. His big shoulders looked like the front bumper of a hummer as he bared down on her.

At the last second, a mop handle crashed into Ted's face and splintered. The end of the handle rattled against the cinder block walls and concrete floor.

Ted cradled his face, and blood gushed from his nose and mouth. He slipped in Johnny's blood as he tried to stand. About the time he gained steady purchase, Steve drove the sharp, broken mop handle into the man's wide-open mouth. He fell over and gurgled as he died.

"That's my man," Angie said.

"I always hated that son of a bitch," he recalled. "Come on."

They hurried down the hall and into the office they met Arthur in to tell him they needed to leave. On the desk, a ledger with all the names of the community sat.

Steve flipped through it. In one of the marked off sections, there was a note saying Arthur deposited a check into the community's account for a million dollars. The money didn't surprise him. He gave all his life savings to the cause decades ago and was sure other wealthy people had done the same when they joined. This check wasn't from a member, however. It was from the U.S. Government. The memo read: For MKUltra Studies

"Look at this, Angie." He pointed to the note. "Why are they sending money?"

"Who cares?"

"I find it interesting. There's no way they fund this type of thing."

He flipped through more of the section. A couple member's contribution to Green's Bay caught him off guard. He would've never guessed that Jack Williamston would've been successful enough to give over two million dollars to the community, nor did he think Jan was his wife when they joined. He had never seen them speak or even acknowledge each other.

"There's so much information here," Steve said. Astonishment dominated his tone.

"There's nothing there I give a damn about," Angie shot back. "I don't need to know how this place runs. I'm leaving."

"I know, I know, but it is interesting. Why is he getting, like, four mil a year from the United States? That's a big deal. We could get him shut down if they knew what was going on."

"I'm shutting him down tonight, one way or another."

"I got it, Angie. I'm just curious."

"I'm sorry. I don't mean to be short with you. I'm just focused."

"You're fine, babe. Let's get it done." Steve smacked her on the ass and kissed her head.

Angie had a tiny giggle escape her. Somehow, that moment took some of the tension and edge off. They just killed four people, and they were running for their lives, but some smiles and a loving moment reminded the two what it was for. It slowed them down and made them remember their love for each other, the good times they've had, and were fighting for in the future. Most of all: their unborn child.

Angie led the way through the little therapist area. There was an oval coffee table, a fake leather chair with studded armrests, and an ugly blue and gray couch with cushions no more than three inches thick. A dusty fabric plant with a wicker basket pot dressed either side of the couch, and a glossy, brown coffee urn sat on the table.

"What you think is in that cabinet?" Steve pointed in the corner. There was a silver cabinet with a clouded glass front fastened to the wall. It was only two feet wide and two feet tall. The style seemed too new to fit the rest of the hospital's décor.

"Nothing we're looking for," Angie said. "Why does it matter?"

Steve's shoulders slumped a bit, like a kid that had just been told he couldn't play with his friends until he finished his homework or couldn't have desert unless he had his gross vegetables.

"Might be something of use in there. That's all. I don't think being too prepared is going to be our issue, so anything that can help would be nice."

He slid the door in its track to the left. Inside, there were several vials with different liquids inside. There was some made for knocking people out, speeding up their heart rates, and even some insulin. On the shelf above the tiny bottles were some syringes and a thick, long rubber band.

"Find the answer?" said Angie. Her smartass tone both irritated Steve and made him laugh.

"You know, the magical land of Narnia." He shot her a playful look.

"What's that on the other side?" She pointed to the part of the cabinet obscured by the sliding door.

Steve shifted it over to the right, and on the top shelf was a pristine scalpel.

"Get that. We may have a use for it," Angie said.

"I wonder how many people went through shit like us, and we never knew it? Arthur's a monster, and I never saw it. I feel foolish."

"I feel far more than just foolish. I think if everyone's eyes were opened—and not the way he likes to say so—they would all feel several emotions. Right now, all I feel is anger. An anger so deep I can't imagine feeling anything ever again."

They stood in silence for a while. Steve thought moving along from the statement without giving its weight a proper acknowledgment would've came across as thoughtless or oblivious. He felt the anger, too. His remained mired down with the fear plaguing him from the beginning. Killing a man he used to hate didn't erase the fear; it made him question the lengths he was willing to go for his woman and stolen child. What worried him more was how the hate came rolling to the top so quickly. Over time, he learned to stuff it down. Letting it go was so ... liberating.

"Let's move on," he said. There was a part of him that felt good about him being the one to say it. It gave him a bit of equal standing with Angie. The shift in power and force had not been lost on him. The opposite roles had been built in for so long that he didn't know how to handle or process things.

She smiled at him. "I've never been happier to."

They worked their way to the back of the room, behind the half wall the desk in the front room sat against. There was a door leading into Arthur's bedroom, so they were careful approaching it.

"You ready?" Angie mouthed.

Steve nodded.

He kicked the door open. Splinters flew from the jamb. The door swung into the wall behind it hard enough to break the lock.

Steve blitzed the room, ready for anything, from any direction in the close quarters. There was an unmade bed, a roll top desk, a dresser, and an overflowing bookcase, but there was no Arthur.

"Hmm ... where would he be this time of

night?" Steve said.

"Damn good question. I wonder if this is normal or has he been alerted?"

"It would've had to be quick to reach him. I think he was already out." Steve put his hands on the bed. "The bed isn't warm at all."

"That's not concerning at all," Angie smirked.

Steve looked around the room. He flipped the covers of the bed back, shuffled through the first couple of drawers in the dresser, and ran his finger along a handful of books on the shelf. When he turned his head sideways, he pulled one down. The bookcase was so full none of the books tilted. They slid sideways, like they were happy to breathe.

"The old man has an interesting taste in literature."

"What is it?"

"The Benefits of Cannibalism." Steve flipped through the pages. "He's pretty interested in the effects of eating brain."

"Oh God." Angie's face was a disgusted mask. "Put that away."

"What's this?" Steve fidgeted with the side of the bookcase.

"What now? I'm ready to get out of here."

He continued jiggling something on the side closest to the barrier wall. His motions became more exaggerated the noise he made grew louder.

"I think .... It's like ... there's ...," there was a metallic pop and the bookcase dropped slightly on one side. "That's what I was thinking."

Steve stepped back, and the bookcase swung away from the wall on one side. Hinges creaked on the wall. A soft beam of fluorescent light filled the opening behind the bookcase.

"Damn. Good catch, babe. What's back there?" said Angie.

"I'm not sure what's at the bottom, but there's a staircase right here."

They descended the stairs with caution. Each step closer to an unseen fate was slower and quieter than the one before. Every noise sounded like an air horn in their ears. Bumps sounded like thunder. Their steps were a hammer on an anvil.

Steve stopped and faced Angie. "I can see the bottom," he whispered. Even that sounded like a shriek. "Be careful."

She nodded.

Steve took the last few steps down. As soon as his foot touched the floor, a row of red siren lights began twirling all the way down a long hallway. Loud buzzing echoed in his ears, and a lanky figure stood in the corridor about twenty feet away, unnatural lines defining it in the siren lights.

"It was a good try, but this is as far as you two get," said the figure. It was Conner. Of course, it would be Conner.

"I have waited a long time to tell you to go fuck yourself," Steve said.

"I always knew you were a pussy. I'm glad I never wasted time respecting you as a man. You and that whore you bred should've been serving me lemonade hand in hand this whole time."

Steve stomped down the hallway toward Conner. "I've heard you and that old asshole put my woman down as much as I plan to."

Steve pulled the scalpel from his pocket as he drew near. He gripped it tightly and attacked Conner.

The scalpel sliced through Conner's raised forearm that was being used as protection. Blood spurted instantly. If Conner felt it, he didn't show it. He punched Steve so hard two of his teeth flew from his mouth.

While Steve was on one knee, Conner brought a double ax-handle blow on his temple. Steve crumbled at the young man's feet.

Conner was so full of adrenaline veins popped from his neck. He screamed a primal cry of victory, one that would rival a dominant lion in the jungle standing over his prey.

"Come on, bitch," he yelled at Steve, who

was crawling away from him. "Get up. You want to talk like a man, you need to fight like one, too."

"I'm not," Angie said from the shadow between two siren beams she'd sneaked to and stabbed him in the throat with the kitchen knife. Never letting go of the knife's handle, she kicked the gurgling man away, then dove on his wilting body stabbing every inch of Conner she could reach. She didn't stop until they were both covered in his blood, and Conner lay, many wounds before, expired.

"Are you okay?" Angie bent down to check on a battered Steve. He reached out to the wall and her pant leg, disoriented.

"He is the least of your problems," called Arthur from down the hall. His voice meshed with the shrill siren to make him sound like they were spoken by a demon.

"Damn right, he is," she replied. Fear, anger, and pure desire to see nothing but the old man suffer ran through her body, but her legs marched straight toward him.

Knowing that Arthur could, and would, kill her didn't deter anything in her mind. She couldn't imagine a single cell in her body that wanted anything more than to be bathed by the man's blood and tears and screams of pain. Every bit of her was focused on reckoning for her child. The saying, *Hell hath no fury like a woman scorned*, failed to include a childless mother.

"You would do best to stop and think about what you're doing," Arthur threatened.

Angie never slowed. If anything, the old man's voice made her long for violence and savagery. He didn't impose a moment of pause for her. Instead, he fueled her hatred.

Even though she wanted to respond to his threat with some kind quick-witted comeback, or something cool she'd seen in similar situations in movies, her lips were glued. She heard everything like it funneled straight to her ears. She felt all her surroundings, to the point the siren rubbed the inside of her chest bone like sandpaper. Her eyes were laser focused on the man that killed and tortured her unborn child, as he stood in the hall, splashed with fading and flashing red light.

"I warned you," Arthur almost chuckled at her. And hell ran through her veins with such veracity that they seared inside her skin.

"I fucking hate you!" she screamed so hard at him her throat popped and began bleeding. It hurt, and she didn't care one tiny bit. She raised the knife above her head and ran at Arthur.

Arthur's hand rose from his waist, and a snub-nosed derringer rang out two shots, both of which hit Angie. One landed high on the outside of her thigh, and the other pierced her shoulder.

The one in her shoulder didn't register, but the one in the thigh caused her to stumble before tripping to the floor. The knife slid past Arthur, and Angie came to rest at the toes of his shoes. She hated him so much and wanted to hurt him. She grabbed his foot and bit as hard as she could through the shoe.

"Hey, you crazy bitch! You have lost your mind!" He tried to pull his foot from her, but she had a crocodile vice on his toe.

Arthur pulled, and finally pushed, like he was kicking, but with her attached. One of the thrusts busted her lips, and the jerk away ripped her two top and bottom front teeth out. After he was freed, he kicked her with the other foot.

"I hate having to kill members of my community. It seems so futile to have given so much of yourself to a group of people who doesn't appreciate it at all. I wonder why I even try sometimes." Arthur loaded two more bullets into the little gun while he spoke. "You should be thanking me right now."

"Wha...." Angie couldn't grasp his words. Pain, rage, and disappointment were the only things making sense.

"For working so hard to save your useless, tainted soul!" he shouted. "How much clearer do I need to be for you? You are the dumbest slash I've ever known. Poor Conner. Now, I understand why he lost his temper with you."

Angie heard him and spit a mouth full of blood on his pants. "I fuckin' hate you."

"Yes, I know. We've covered that. If you quit living in the past, like replaying that ugly, shriveled abomination you called your child in your mind. I gave you a gift of learning. A lesson. And here you are, still clinging to a memory and a wish. This is why you can't be given power to make decisions, nor can those who have like-minded objectives."

Angie pressed her upper body up and slid her knees beneath her. She sat up and stared Arthur in the face. "I ... fuckin' ... hate ...."

"Me, I know," Arthur cut her sentence off. "I'm not as dumb as you or your asshole lover."

Arthur pulled the hammer back on the derringer. The click was surprisingly loud to Angie given the siren roaring, but the barrel rested on her face. She could feel the machine work inside popping.

"Just like your offspring, you'll die by my hand," Arthur smiled.

Angie ripped the meat cleaver from her waistband and thrust it upward into Arthur's crotch.

The gun fired twice, but over Angie's head, and sparks flew where the bullets ricocheted off the floor. Immense pain erupted within Arthur. He dropped the gun and held his wound. His face was a mask of surprise, mere inches from Angie's. She swirled her tongue in her mouth and spat in his face. Blood ran down his face like paint on a wall.

Angie jerked the cleaver from Arthur's body and slammed it back in. She put every ounce of weight she could behind the blows and only felt bad that she couldn't do it harder.

Arthur fell on top of her, blood pouring from his mangled genitals. She shrugged his quivering body off her shoulders and spun to get an angle to continue.

His hands tried to cover her attack area, but she stabbed through them, crushing and slicing through his fingers. The force behind her strikes shattered his bones and knuckles. Chunks of meat flew from his body like gruesome confetti.

Screams of pain filled the corridor. Screams of unabashed hostility and frustration matched their intensity. Sweat and blood covered Angie like a blanket. Her heart raced so rapidly she felt it struggling to pump. She thought if she died from killing Arthur, she would die happy.

Then a voice pulled her back. "It's done, babe. Stop."

Steve touched her leg, having worked

himself all the way to them on his hands and knees. His lips, chin, and chest were covered in blood. His eyes were still dilated, but recognition of her was apparent on his face.

"It's okay," he said. "It's over."

She dropped the cleaver and tugged the torch from her pants. It sputtered to life, and she put the end of the flame to Arthur's shirt. The blue fire danced up his body, and soon, his corpse was a mound of burning flesh.

Angie's arms slackened, and her shoulders dropped. Tears spilled from her eyes, and she sniffled, refusing to outwardly sob.

"Let's go. There's a door at the end of this hall. It says it's an exit," Steve said.

They helped each other to their feet and limped toward the door. Angie felt every muscle in her body loosen tension. She thought she may fall apart when they did. Her mouth was so swollen she was sure it would explode if it weren't already busted. But, she avenged her baby's murder. A woman, the inferior gender, the group that are only good enough to serve man, killed him. *She* taught him a lesson.

"What are you cooking?" Steve said, calling through the living room into the kitchen.

Their new house was quaint and just right for them. After they broke free of the community, they traveled through three towns in West Africa before they went to the hospital. When they were asked what happened, they said they were robbed. They were aware of the fact that telling on the remaining cult members would also alert them to the couple's location. That was the last thing either of them wanted.

They moved back to America after healing. After so long in the hot, dry weather, they wanted a place with a winter, and precipitation. They chose Ohio.

Steve got a job at a local mail office. He made pretty good money and had health benefits. Angie picked up a few spots a week helping a cleaning company when they needed it. Life was good.

"Hamburgers," Angie said. "It's our anniversary."

"Damn, it is. I hadn't even thought about it. I'm sorry."

"Don't be silly. It's nothing big."

He sat at the table and shuffled through the adverts and envelopes he'd brought in from the mailbox. All of a sudden, he jumped back from the table, like he'd grabbed a snake. The chair tipped and tripped him, knocking him on his ass against the wall.

"What the hell is wrong?" Angie yelled.

Steve scrambled to his feet and pointed to the pile of mail. An envelope sat facing Angie. A familiar logo in green ink said, *Be free at Green's Bay Community.*

About the Author

Known as the Southern Tale Spinner, T.S. Woolard is an American author from the pines of North Carolina. Well known for his horror and poetry, Woolard has been gaining notoriety in the Indie community as his unique style enraptures the masses. Published in numerous anthologies by both JWK Publishing and JEA Publishing, as well as having personal writings published with the two companies, Solo Circus and The

Meaning of Hell, his exposure began. Previously published with Siren's Call ezine, and now a current author with Dark Moon Rising Publications, Woolard has taken Indie publishing by storm. Woolard's latest release, Heaven's Healer from Hell, is a taste as to what my short story collections are all about. With one novel, one novella, 2 short story collections, and a poetry book out on the market, Woolard has yet to slow down as he gains ground with new fans each day. Woolard's work is available at Amazon and all other major book outlets.

Follow him on Twitter @TSWoolard.
Follow him on Instagram @TSwoolard
Follow him on Facebook @writertswoolard

CPSIA information can be obtained
at www.ICGtesting.com
Printed in the USA
LVHW090822010920
664633LV00004B/468